She's about to live out her wildest fantasy...

For the first time since she'd met Noah, Ari didn't feel any of the negative tension—only the sexual kind now. Her reaction to him just proved that she didn't have to like him to want to do him.

"I was hoping we could have dinner together soon. Maybe tonight?" Noah said.

"Sure," she said. Why was everything she wanted suddenly falling into her lap now so easily? There had to be a catch. Maybe she wasn't really ready to proposition the guy who'd been the object of so many of her sexual fantasies.

As soon as she was out of Noah's office, walking home, she knew what the catch was—she was going to be the next woman in his window.

Dear Reader,

What would you do if you had a neighbor who liked to perform indiscreet acts in front of his open window, for all the world to see? Would you draw the shades, or would you pop some popcorn and pull up a chair for the show? When the heroine of *Made You Look* is presented with this dilemma, she watches, and watches, and watches some more.

I live in an apartment building similar to the heroine's, with another building across the way, and I've often wondered how many eyes are watching me when I accidentally leave a curtain open. And I can see into other people's apartments as easily as they can see into mine. Lucky for my neighbors, I have a natural instinct to honor other people's privacy. Otherwise, they might find their lives serving as fodder for fiction.

Unfortunately, I haven't ever seen anything remotely interesting happening through an open window, even accidentally. Which is why I write fiction—I can create a world where there's always something fascinating happening in the open window.

I hope you enjoy *Made You Look*. You can learn more about me and my upcoming books at www.jamiesobrato.com.

Sincerely,

Jamie Sobrato

Jamie Sobrato

MADE YOU LOOK

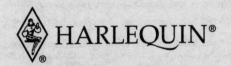

TORONTO • NEW YORK • LONDON
AMSTERDAM • PARIS • SYDNEY • HAMBURG
STOCKHOLM • ATHENS • TOKYO • MILAN • MADRID
PRAGUE • WARSAW • BUDAPEST • AUCKLAND

Recycling programs
for this product may
not exist in your area.

ISBN-13: 978-0-373-79494-2

MADE YOU LOOK

Copyright © 2009 by Jamie Sobrato.

This edition published by arrangement with Harlequin Books S.A.

® and TM are trademarks of the publisher. Trademarks indicated with ® are registered in the United States Patent and Trademark Office, the Canadian Trade Marks Office and in other countries.

www.eHarlequin.com

Printed in U.S.A.

ABOUT THE AUTHOR

Jamie Sobrato has dreamed of being a writer ever since composing her first bad poetry at the age of eight. *Made You Look* is the eighteenth book she has written for Harlequin Books. Jamie lives in Northern California with her two kids and a small zoo of animals. Unlike the heroine in this novel, she never, ever spies on her neighbors—especially not with binoculars.

Books by Jamie Sobrato

Don't miss any of our special offers. Write to us at the following address for information on our newest releases.

Harlequin Reader Service
U.S.: 3010 Walden Ave., P.O. Box 1325, Buffalo, NY 14269
Canadian: P.O. Box 609, Fort Erie, Ont. L2A 5X3

To Wanda Ottewell, editor extraordinaire

1

THEY WERE AT IT AGAIN.

She could see them through her window, in the penthouse across the way. Bare skin, a tangle of taut, beautiful limbs—impossible not to notice.

Out of habit, Ari picked up her binoculars and brought them to her eyes. Instantly, she had an intimate view of her neighbor's body parts. She turned slightly to adjust and found herself staring at a hand—his hand—traveling up the outside of a curvaceous thigh.

Up, up, up it went, stopping at the flare of her hips, where he grasped firmly. Ari adjusted the binoculars again, and she had a view of a shoulder, then his mouth, kissing the delicate flesh of her neck.

His expression was intense, determined. He was solely focused on the task—no, make that the woman—at hand. And as always, for reasons she couldn't quite explain, Ari found herself wishing that woman was her. She didn't really want to be with a man, and there was nothing about this man in particular that made him seem exactly like her type, but she did want to feel what that woman must have been feeling at that moment. Ari wanted to feel desire, intimacy, skin-on-skin contact, sensual pleasure—all things missing from her life for the past two years.

Her body responded to the scene with a warming down low, a delicious ache she didn't get to feel often these days. Well, except when watching her overly amorous neighbor.

To the window seat, every time.

And it wasn't like in this neighborhood of apartment buildings and condos, he was mistaking his view for a private one. At any given moment, scores of people could be watching him get it on with whichever of his latest conquests he'd brought home for the evening.

Tonight, she was a beautiful, voluptuous blonde, though something about her perfect hair suggested she lived in the Marina District. She probably had a dog she loved more than her own mother, drove a late-model BMW and worked for a biotech start-up, or maybe a downtown investment firm.

Ari knew the type.

She almost felt sorry for the endless stream of girls Sir Sex-a-Lot, as she liked to call him, invited in and out of his life. Seriously, could he really have gotten them all to go to bed with him without at least alluding to the chance that they might have a real relationship?

Doubtful.

Well, okay, maybe she was being a wee bit judgmental. Probably because she wasn't getting laid herself, and it was making her cranky these days.

At times, she had to admit, the reason she watched Sex-a-Lot's exploits was that it got her off. And maybe it was his whorish behavior that made him the ideal random guy for her to fantasize about—her dirty little clean-cut businessman fantasy. Nothing was going to happen with him, and he obviously didn't mind being objectified, so he was safe, distant and available.

She didn't have a sex life of her own anymore, and his was

the next closest one to get any entertainment from. And, since he was basically inviting her to watch anyway...

But pleasuring herself to the image of another couple's lovemaking no longer sounded like any fun at all—if it ever had. She was thirty-two years old, and her dance career was faltering as she devoted more and more of her time to the dinner club she'd bought eight years ago, and tonight standing here with her binoculars only made her feel pathetic.

Angry, frustrated, alone. It was as if nothing satisfied her anymore. Not even her cheap, reliable thrills.

She lowered the binoculars, dropped them on the purple velvet sofa and slouched down next to where they landed, still watching the couple across the way get it on. But she no longer had the warm buzzing sensation down low. She only felt empty.

And this, perhaps, was the final insult.

It had been two miserable years ago today, she'd realized when she'd checked her schedule on the calendar that morning. Two years since her life had started falling apart. Two years since one horrid, vile assault in an alley had stolen who she used to be and transformed her into this woman who was no longer someone she recognized.

Ari closed her eyes, and she recalled in a flash how it had all gone down. The struggle, the fear, the haunting sense of invasion.

Two years, and she could still remember as if it had happened yesterday.

Who was this person she'd become? Scared of life, scared of men, scared of herself. Hiding behind a workaholic job that didn't fulfill her. She was supposed to be a dancer, not a business owner. She was supposed to be a sensual being, not a monk.

It was only when she felt tears drip onto her chest that she realized she was crying. Silent, streaming tears fell down her cheeks and soaked the low neckline of her black top. She didn't bother wiping them away. When she thought of the calendar again, a cry escaped her throat, and she doubled over onto the dark red rug her mother had brought from Turkey, letting the racking sobs come out now, the ones that had been threatening to escape for so long she'd forgotten to be on guard against them.

But she let it all out now, every moan, every sob, every cry of rage and grief she'd been holding in. She let it out until there was nothing left, and her tears were merely a trickle.

When she pulled herself up off the floor, the couple across the way were no longer in the window, thank God.

She could see instead, when she looked out at the fog settling on the cool San Francisco night, a vision of her life without the baggage she carried now, a vision of her life as it was supposed to be, not as it was.

She knew, finally, what she needed to do to heal.

But first, she had a lot of work to do.

One month later...

"HAVE YOU LOST your freaking mind? You can't sell Cabaret. It's a San Francisco institution!"

This was not the response Ari was hoping for from her business broker of choice. The fact that her would-be agent was also a longtime friend did make her somewhat biased, but still. She winced at Cara's response and braced herself to defend her decision.

"I've been thinking about this for some time—it's not a rash decision," Ari said calmly as she crossed her living room, the phone pressed to her ear. "I've also spent the past month getting the place in spotless shape, all polished and ready to sell."

"But it won't be the same without you."

"Whoever buys it will want to keep it as it is, so Cabaret will live on, I'm sure."

"You can't guarantee that the new owner will keep the place as is."

"I can make it a condition of sale, can't I?"

Over the phone, she could hear Cara sigh heavily. "I guess you can try, but—"

"Look, here's what I need from you," Ari said. "Sound confident. Tell me I can do this."

"Um… What exactly am I supposed to be telling you that you can do?"

"That I can sell Cabaret and everything will be fine. I love the place, but I have to get out from under it. It's a time sink, and it's turned me into boring-ass businesswoman. That's not *me*."

"I guess you're right."

"You know I'm right! I'm a dancer. That's what I want to be doing."

"But—"

"I'm burned out, Cara. I need to get back to focusing on what I love."

"Which is what? Ruining my favorite hangouts? You dance at Cabaret."

"No, I *used* to dance. Now I spend ninety percent of my time running the place, and it's not fun. It's not me. I'm losing myself."

Cara sighed again.

Ari didn't want to mention the other reason she had to sell the place, but Cara was going to guess sooner or later.

"Also, I just… I can't… I feel like maybe a change will help me put the past to rest."

As she spoke, she looked out the window at her neighbor's apartment, which was empty now. She hadn't let herself watch him again since the night she'd broken down crying. She'd even gone so far as to keep her curtains drawn most of the time.

The last sentence she'd spoken hung in the air, creating an awkward silence. Then Cara recovered.

"Right," she said. "I understand. I do. I just hate to see you throw away financial security."

"I'm not. I'm going to keep the building and lease it to the next owner. I'll earn enough from the rent alone to keep me comfortable, and I'll start teaching dance classes in the studio space upstairs."

She'd inherited the building from her father eight years ago when he'd died of a heart attack, and that sad event had been the impetus for her starting Cabaret. Now another sad event was going to be the reason she let the business go. At least she'd still own the building.

"Sounds like you've thought this through pretty thoroughly."

"I have. Now it's just the matter of finding a buyer for the business. And the right agent. I was hoping you'd help me sell the place."

"Of course I will," Cara said. "It's going to be no small task, finding the right buyer, though."

Ari knew her friend was simply being practical, but she didn't want to hear any discouraging words right now. She wanted to believe she could really move on from the business quickly, that she wouldn't have to linger around the memories of it for too long.

Cara continued, still sounding doubtful. "Don't you worry that being in the upstairs studio will still be too close for comfort…to the alley?"

Ari refused to feel sick at the mention of the alley. She was past reacting emotionally now.

"Yeah," Ari said quietly, "I'll still have to see it if I look out the window. But it won't be as bad as closing down the restaurant late at night. Every time I have to do that, it brings back memories of that night, and…"

"I get it. Teaching dance, you'll never be there late and alone, right?"

"Exactly."

"Did you ever call my therapist and make an appointment?"

"Not yet," Ari answered. "I haven't had time."

And she never would.

Cara sighed heavily. She'd been pushing Ari to see one ever since she'd confided what had happened. But Ari didn't like therapists, and she didn't want to believe that her problems were too big for her to solve herself. She'd grown up watching her mother visit therapist after therapist, dragging in their whole family at times, and it never helped a damn thing. As far as Ari could tell, it only made her mother and their family worse off—victims of their own helplessness.

She wasn't going to fall into that trap. Ari had vowed, two years and one month ago, that she would never be a victim again.

"Okay," Cara said. "We'll make it happen. We'll get you out from under Cabaret."

"Thank you. I needed to hear that."

Ari felt tension draining from her shoulders. Hearing someone else say it felt one step closer to making it happen.

And freeing herself from Cabaret would be one step closer to freeing herself, period. From her past, from her unwanted responsibilities, from whatever last bit of grief that was weighing her down.

2

"LIZ CALLED while you were gone. Also, Jacey or Tracy, and some other chick whose name I forgot."

Noah Kellerman stopped in his tracks and frowned at his little brother's words. "Who's *Liz?*"

"I didn't ask her to fax over a résumé." Simon looked back at the TV and sank deeper into the sofa, where he apparently intended to spend the whole day.

"I don't think I know a Liz."

"Maybe you ought to consider asking for names before you go putting your dick inside anyone."

Noah dropped the mail on the table and took off his shoes and coat.

"You've got such an elegant way with words."

"I call it like I see it, bro. You're like an addict when it comes to sex."

Noah didn't like his brother's insinuation, but the moment he opened his mouth to protest, he realized he'd sound like a hypocrite if he did.

And he had more important things to consider than his own sexual proclivities. He'd just heard from his real estate agent that she'd e-mailed him a property she was looking into for him.

He went to his computer, booted it up and checked his e-mail.

There it was.

Successful, well-known San Francisco dinner club, 6000 square feet to be leased from seller at $6,500 monthly rent; liquor license and full bar; space equipped with stage, kitchen with all appliances; popular North Beach neighborhood with high foot traffic.

Exactly what he was looking for. His heart raced.

He'd heard rumors that Cabaret—the only place in North Beach that fit this description—was going to be put on the market. It was exactly the kind of place that was ripe for the transformation he had in mind.

Noah leaned forward in his leather desk chair and read over the sale listing again, just to make sure his eyes hadn't fooled him.

"I think I've found it," he said.

"Found what?" Simon asked, as he flipped idly through channels on the plasma TV.

"The restaurant we've been looking for."

"If by *we,* you mean *you,* then more power to ya."

Aside from his art, which didn't earn him any money, Simon had the ambition of a tree slug, as evidenced by his semipermanent residence on Noah's white, postmodern Roche Bobois sofa, which was not the kind of seat meant for days on end of eating Cheetos and watching reality TV. Thank God the leather tended to allow the wiping-off of tell-tale orange crumbs.

"This is your key to employment success, little brother. Remember, I won't fire you for all the reasons you usually get fired."

"My motto is Do Less, Be More."'"

"That's great if you can find a Zen Buddhist way to pay

the rent. Until you do, you're going to have to take the breaks you can get."

Noah had been supporting Simon most of their lives, even when they'd had a mother around to theoretically do the supporting. But he was determined to give his little brother the sense of responsibility and pride that came with self-sufficiency, one way or another. Simon may be bipolar, but that didn't mean he was helpless.

When his brother wasn't watching sometimes—like now, when his attention was riveted to an episode of an inane talk show—Noah would stare at his profile until his eyes blurred and he could see their mother sitting there instead. Simon had their mother's dark hair and slight build, her nose and her chin, too. He was her child right down to the kind of medication he needed to function properly.

Noah missed their mother at odd times like this, missed the rare glimpses he'd had of the woman she might have been if she'd been dealt a better lot in life, and these moments felt like a hard kick in the chest.

He hated that his memories of her always brought on a barrage of conflicted emotions. He'd been embarrassed by her as a kid, humiliated by their poverty, terrified of her instability. And at the core of it all was the fact that he'd loved her with the intensity of a child who had only one parent.

And Simon, at his worst, was a painful reminder of their mother's too-frequent bad decisions, the ones that left them kicked out of their apartments, homeless and broke. It made Noah doubly diligent in ensuring his brother got the care and support he needed, where their mother never had.

Yeah, there was the guilt that he hadn't been able to take care of her, too. That never went away.

Instead of dwelling on the negative feelings, he cleared

his throat and turned his attention back to the computer, back to the prospect of buying the business that would be his masterpiece.

Ever since buying his first hot dog stand at the age of eighteen with money he'd saved working as a busboy at a popular L.A. restaurant, Noah had been maneuvering his way toward this moment. He'd turned the hot dog stand into the only gourmet dog spot in L.A. He'd sold it for a nice profit, and with that money he'd been able to get a loan for a failing diner in a not-yet-gentrified part of the city. He'd turned it into the hippest place to be seen having a middle-of-the-night breakfast after the clubs closed down.

Then he'd sold the diner and used the profits to buy and transform a seedy seafood restaurant into a four-star-rated must-visit spot for Asian fusion cuisine.

But his heart had never completely been in it. Ever since his busboy job, he'd had a vision of the place he wanted to create, and he'd needed to get away from all the bad memories of L.A. in order to do it. San Francisco was the place, with its air of reinvention, its nostalgia and its culture of great food. And, he had a gut feeling he'd just found his restaurant.

He wanted to see the place again. He'd walked past and even been inside once before, but he hadn't taken a close look. Now he wanted to see with his own eyes, reimagine the place as he would make it and check out the employees, the operations, the surrounding neighborhood—whatever he might use to factor into his offer.

In fact, he was going there right now to check it out. If the perfect property really had come on the market, he wanted to act fast.

A quick Internet search confirmed that the restaurant opened at five, which meant there would be at least a few people on site prepping for the evening, and the club was only a ten- or fifteen-minute walk from his penthouse.

"I'm going out for a bit. See you later," he said to the back of Simon's head.

"Later, man," Simon called after him as he walked out the door to the elevator.

In the lobby, he noticed out the window that a light drizzle had started to fall. And as he stepped out into the early evening, the cool, wet air enveloped him and reminded him of yet another reason he loved the city. There was a sense of timelessness here, of one day, one month, one season, one year, blending into another.

Unlike L.A., where he'd grown up, the seasons here were not divided by hot, dry summers and rainy winters. There simply were no distinct seasons, at least not unless one observed closely.

A quick downhill walk toward the ocean brought Noah to the front of Cabaret. Overhead, its red neon sign shouted the restaurant's name in a script that managed to look both feminine and tawdry. That would have to go, along with the name itself. He didn't care how tongue-in-cheek, trashy-hip Cabaret's image was, he envisioned a whole different image—and name. A subtle, minimalist take on Art Deco, perhaps. Something that would suggest both elegance and a fresh twist on the dinner clubs of old.

But he was getting ahead of himself. First he had to buy the business.

He pushed the brass-handled door open and stepped into the lobby. An unstaffed host station divided the lobby from the rest of the space, and beyond it, there were empty tables, a bar off to the right and, on the far side, a stage. There was a woman behind the bar prepping for the evening, and several people in the area of the stage—one in front sweeping, and a woman whom he could hardly take his eyes off rehearsing dance moves to the sounds of some sort of Middle Eastern fusion music with a heavy drumbeat.

She had the long, lean lines of a dancer, but they were softened by the voluptuous curves of her hips and chest. Long, dark, wavy hair that she'd pulled into a ponytail cascaded down her back, swaying with her movements. Her skin, a pale olive tone, glowed in the soft lighting.

Her feet were bare, but she wore a pair of black pants that hugged her thighs, and a black stretchy tank top that made it hard not to stare at her chest. As she danced, the movements of her hips, wrapped in a purple scarf adorned with dangling gold coins, were blatantly sexual. Noah forced himself to look away to avoid getting turned-on.

Instead, he surveyed his surroundings. The dark red carpet, the gilded chairs with purple and green velvet cushions, the funky antique tables, the ornate crystal chandeliers—it would all have to go.

He needed to figure out if there was a manager on duty so he could ask a few questions. He didn't intend to admit he was interested in buying the place—that was his business broker's job—but he did want to poke around and get a better sense of how it was being run.

Noah approached the guy sweeping. "Excuse me," Noah said.

He stopped his work and looked up. "Hey, sorry, but we're closed right now."

"I was just wondering if you have a listing of upcoming shows."

The man nodded. He was in his late twenties perhaps, his arms covered in tattoos and his head shaved. He had several piercings on each ear, and one on his tongue. His image was pretty much the opposite of what Noah would be looking for in employees.

"Sure, you can always check our Web site. And there're flyers there in the lobby." He pointed to a stack of red papers on top of the host's station.

"Which show do you recommend?" Noah asked, buying himself some time.

He didn't want to leave now, not when the woman was still dancing. Something about her made it hard to walk away, as if like a moon he was pulled into her planetary orbit.

"If it's your first time, you can't go wrong with the Araby show—it's the one that made us famous."

Noah already knew this from having read a review in the newspaper, but he nodded as if it was news to him. "Are you the manager here?"

"Nope, I work maintenance. If you need to talk to someone in charge, there's your lady up there." He gestured to the woman onstage.

"And her name is?"

"Arianna Day. She owns the place. You can have a seat and wait for her to finish rehearsing if you want to talk."

The tattooed guy picked up his broom and headed for the kitchen, but before Noah could sit down, the music stopped and the woman onstage turned her attention to Noah.

"Is there something I can help you with?" she asked as she descended the stairs.

Her voice, somehow both sexy and crisp, caught him off guard. She had the sort of tone that could get a guy instantly attracted over the phone. Noah forgot what he'd planned on asking her.

"You're Arianna?"

"Yes," she said, and he detected a note of wariness. She

stopped in front of him but didn't extend her hand. "Who's asking?"

He held out his own hand, but she simply stared down at it, then back at his face.

"I don't need a water purification system," she said flatly, "if that's what you're selling."

The last time he'd gotten such a chilly reception when meeting someone new was a few months ago when he'd accidentally backed his car into the front bumper of a brand-new Maserati.

He resisted the temptation to defend himself against the claim that he was a salesman, made a mental note to get rid of the jacket he was wearing and shrugged. "Fair enough. Do you happen to have any friends who might need water purification systems?"

She crossed her arms over her lovely chest and glared at him. "Perhaps you missed the No Soliciting sign on the front window."

He smiled and held up his hands in mock defeat. "I'm sorry. I'll take my peddling elsewhere."

No sense, after all, in giving away his reason for being there. He'd gathered enough information for now. He knew that the place would need a complete remodel, probably half the employees would have to be canned and Arianna Day needed a serious attitude adjustment.

Good thing he knew how to play hardball better than anyone he'd ever met.

"WE HAVE AN OFFER."

Ari recognized immediately the sound of Cara's voice. She realized after a moment that she was holding her breath, so she exhaled and said, "Okay?"

"Don't sound so afraid. It's a good one. I'm downstairs right now. Are you home?"

"Yes! Get up here!"

It all felt so fast. They'd only placed the restaurant on the market yesterday. And they had an offer today? *Already?*

She hung up the phone and hurried to the front door to unlock it. Then she grabbed the mail from the couch and the towel she'd left on the chair that morning and put them both away. A minute later, Cara was standing in the doorway calling out, "Knock, knock…"

Ari smiled and gave her old friend a hug. "Can I get you a drink?"

"Maybe later. Let's sit down and get to the good stuff first."

Ari could hardly believe this moment had come. Although she remained committed to selling Cabaret, she'd still had her doubts. At times she'd feared she wouldn't be able to survive without the income from it, or she'd felt sad that the place might change without her, or she worried that she was making the decision for the wrong reasons. She'd thought she'd have more time to deal with those emotions. But now, faced with the reality that it might really happen, she felt only an overwhelming sense of relief.

Cara smiled at her expectantly as she placed a manila folder of papers on the table. Ari sat in the chair across from her friend.

"Okay, so did we get the full asking price?"

Her smile grew broader. "He's offering asking price plus twenty percent, and another ten percent over any other offers we receive in the next week."

"Wow."

"Yes, wow. And more important, he's got the cash in hand, ready to buy without any financing."

Ari leaned back in her seat as reality sank in.

"You're kidding, right?"

"Nope." Cara shook her head, but something about her expression put Ari on alert.

"So what's the catch?"

Her friend gave her a look. "He's rejecting several of the conditions you've put on the sale."

"Like?"

"He doesn't want to enter into any agreement about how the business will be run once he's taken ownership."

Here was the part she feared most. "You mean he won't agree to keep Cabaret intact?"

"Right. And…he won't agree to guarantee the current employees will keep their jobs."

"So," Ari said, disappointed, "we'll hold out for a better offer."

Cara stared at her for a moment, her expression carefully neutral. She was going into hard-core sales mode.

"Let's go for a walk, okay?" Cara finally said. "We can let things settle a bit before you make any final decisions."

"I don't want to go for a walk." Ari knew she was being surly, but she couldn't help herself.

They'd been friends since college at U.C. Santa Barbara, when Ari had been a performing arts major, and Cara had been a business major with a dance minor. So her friend had seen her worst behavior countless times, and there wasn't any reason to rein herself in now.

"Ari, the economy isn't doing so swimmingly, and cash-in-hand offers are nothing to sneeze at. I need you to think very seriously about this."

"I am. I don't want some asshole in a suit destroying what I've built, what I've poured my heart and soul into for most of my adult life."

"Before you label him an asshole, maybe you should consider meeting him in person and talking to him a bit."

Ari wanted to argue, but the look on her friend's face gave her pause. She was pushing her luck, and maybe she did need to calm down a wee bit before she refused the guy's offer.

"Let's go over to Double Rainbow and get an ice cream. What do you say?"

She couldn't be persuaded with ice cream, but…

"Mmm, turtle fudge… Okay. I'm open to bribery."

Cara sighed, visibly relieved. This was her income, too, after all. Ari had to remember that. She wasn't the only person for whom selling her business mattered a great deal.

The two walked down the four flights of stairs to the street, then took a left and headed toward the neighborhood ice-cream shop a few blocks away.

As they reached the corner stop sign and were waiting to cross, Cara spoke. "You might want to consider a counter offer, regarding the sale conditions."

"Like what?"

"Maybe…if he'll agree to guarantee all current employees a job, pending adequate performance, you'll agree to sell knowing he's going to change the business to a whole new concept."

Ari opened her mouth to argue, but Cara held up a hand.

"Just wait. Don't say anything yet. Think about it."

"You're ruining my appetite for ice cream."

"I'm sorry. I'm a little preoccupied. I told the buyer's agent we'd get back to him by tonight with an answer."

"You can. My response is *no*."

"I'm as disappointed as you are at the idea of Cabaret disappearing. I love that place—as evidenced by the fact that I spend most of my free evenings at the bar there."

"I know," Ari said sullenly.

"However, we have to be realistic."

"I hate that word. If I'd been realistic, I never would have tried to build a business around the concept of a belly dancing troupe. I'd never have become a belly dancer in the first place."

Cara smirked. "No, you'd have become something boring like a business broker."

Ari couldn't help but laugh. "Don't worry, you're the least boring commercial tool I know."

Cara went silent for a few moments, then said, "Even though this is our first potential buyer, in this sluggish market, it's nothing short of a miracle to get a cash-in-hand offer over the selling price right away. He must have had his eye on Cabaret before it even went on the market."

And one of Ari's goals from the start had been a quick sale. Once the second anniversary of her attack rolled around again, she'd realized she wanted to sell the place. Fast.

She went silent as she let the dilemma roll around in her mind.

A few minutes later, they reached the shop and placed their orders. Once they'd each claimed a scoop of ice cream in a cup and found a seat at a booth near the back of the shop, Ari let the taste of chocolate and caramel soothe her. It really did work as a mood enhancer. Instantly, she was feeling better, as though whatever problem she had was manageable. It was a trick she'd learned recently—do whatever was necessary, big or small, to feel better.

Feeling better had become her primary focus in life lately, and selling Cabaret, she knew, would help. She looked across the small table at her friend, who was busy digging out a chunk of cookie dough.

She'd never talked to Cara about how nonexistent her love life had become, but all of a sudden she wondered why. And yet, when she considered talking about it, it was hard to find the right words.

Where to start? Everyone around her had to have noticed that she'd stopped dating, stopped going out, stopped being herself.

And yet, no one nagged her to get out more. No one tried to set her up on blind dates with a friend of a friend. It was as if everyone tiptoed around the fact that she was damaged goods. Which hurt like hell.

"You know," she said to Cara, "once I don't have the responsibility of Cabaret anymore…I'll have more free time, I hope. I've been feeling like maybe…I need to get a life."

Her friend frowned. "You have a perfectly lovely life, don't you?"

"Maybe. I mean, yeah, of course I do."

Now she felt stupid for not being grateful for all she did have. A thriving business, a chance to sell it and focus on her creative passion, good friends, a place to call home…

And yet.

She was lonely.

And it didn't help that the object of her sexual fantasies had walked right into Cabaret yesterday and tried to sell her a water purification system. It was as if the universe was mocking her loneliness. She'd been so appalled to see him there, and under such circumstances—so different from her fantasies of how they might meet—she hadn't been able to react with anything but coldness. Any other response might have sent some kind of signal of what she did with him in her head.

"That's right," Cara said. "You do. I'm envious of you, really."

"That's ridiculous. You earn a huge income and have possibly the coolest apartment of anyone I know. What do you have to envy about me?"

"Oh, come on, to be as gorgeous and talented as you are? What woman wouldn't love the position you're in?"

"Is this a grass-is-greener discussion?"

"I don't know—is it?"

Ari took another bite of ice cream, desperately needing it to work its magic now. She suddenly didn't know what to feel about anything. Was she supposed to be happy with her life exactly like it was? Or was she supposed to want something more?

Wasn't wanting, as her spiritual teacher often pointed out, the source of all unhappiness?

"Do you just need to get laid? Is that the problem?"

If only it were that simple. Well, it was, and it wasn't.

"I need… I don't know what I need."

Cara frowned as she studied her. "You've changed so much."

The naked truth of Cara's statement slapped Ari in the face. "How have I changed?" she asked quietly, though she already knew the answer.

Cara shook her head. "I'm sorry. I don't mean in a bad way. It's just…"

"How have I changed?" Ari demanded.

"You know—you used to be walking sex. You used to turn men's and women's heads wherever you went without even trying. It's part of what gives you such a great stage presence. And you used to love men so much. I really envied how free and uninhibited you were. I remember the first time I saw you dance onstage in college, I understood I didn't have what it took to make it as a dancer. But you did."

"And now?"

"Don't get me wrong. The way you've changed, it's totally

understandable. Anyone would. I mean, you've just…you've withdrawn. You don't radiate sensuality anymore. You've gotten kind of…closed off, I guess."

It was all true. Ari was too stunned to respond.

"The only time I see glimpses of the old Ari is when you're onstage dancing."

Glimpses was the key word there. The only time Ari felt like her old self was onstage, and even then, not all the time. If for even a moment she allowed herself to contemplate that there was an audience, that she was being watched, she would lose that tenuous hold on her confidence and she would feel herself harden, forming a protective shell to keep out what might hurt her.

"I don't want to be closed off anymore."

She braced herself for the therapy recommendation yet again, but Cara surprised her by simply nodding and saying, "Good for you. I think deciding not to be is half the battle."

"And," Ari said, taking a deep breath and exhaling all the tension that had built up inside her, "I think we should give the buyer a new set of conditions."

"What do you have in mind?"

"First, I want to meet him face-to-face to discuss what changes he has in mind."

"Okay," Cara said as she took a notepad and pen out of her purse and began making notes. "I don't know for sure if he'll be open to that, but I'll ask."

Ari decided to look on the bright side. This was an opportunity, not another reason to feel discouraged. She would meet this buyer and she'd turn on her old charm, and he wouldn't stand a chance.

3

NOAH TOOK HIS SEAT at the reserved table, front and center below the Cabaret stage. He'd been surprised by his business broker's call to inform him that the seller wanted to meet him after the show tonight—no agents allowed—and that she was offering him two free tickets, plus dinner and drinks for himself and a guest, so that she could discuss the business with him afterward.

He'd reluctantly agreed, though his businessman's radar had immediately gone on alert. He'd already had one encounter with the bristly owner of Cabaret, and this odd request of hers only hinted further that she wasn't going to be an easy person to deal with. She was angling for something.

And he had to figure out her angle.

The show was about to start, and the lights went dim as a waitress approached him to take his drink order.

"Will anyone be joining you?" she asked after he'd requested a scotch on the rocks.

"A friend will be here any time now. He'll have a gin and tonic."

The pretty blonde, whose name tag read Sophie, smiled at him and nodded, then left the table. Ordinarily, he'd probably have been calculating whether or not he wanted to sleep with the waitress, but not tonight. And he'd considered inviting a date along for the evening, but when he thought of

Arianna Day, he couldn't come up with anyone to invite. Everyone seemed dull and uninteresting compared to the huffy, arrogant owner, so he'd opted instead for his best friend, Tyson, whom he hadn't seen in a few weeks.

He looked at the menu, spotted the filet and decided he'd have that without giving it any further thought.

Glancing around the room, he was both pleased and annoyed to see that the place was packed. It was a Thursday night, but Ari and her troupe were doing a show, and apparently their performances were becoming rarer and rarer. Probably everyone was here to see them while they could.

Part of him didn't want the current business to be so successful that customers were disappointed when he transformed the place into something entirely new. He had never been to one of Cabaret's shows before, but he'd heard the rave reviews. He knew without seeing a minute of it that it wasn't his cup of tea. He didn't go for ironic-trashy, or pseudo-hip, or faux dime-store chic, or any of the other pretentious styles San Francisco thirtysomethings were so fond of.

In that way, he sometimes felt out of place in the city, but feeling out of place was nothing new to him. Growing up homeless half the time and living in tenement apartments and shelters the other half had given him a long, hard schooling in how to be an outsider, always on the wrong side of the window looking in.

Achieving financial success didn't really erase any of those old feelings. Rather, in a cruel twist of fate, it seemed to magnify them. Now he had all the trappings of success, but none of the sense of entitlement, none of the insider experience, none of the history. Unlike most of his peers, he hadn't grown up in a cushy suburban home, attended private schools or gotten a free ride through college from Mom and Dad.

But he also knew that even if his good fortune did vanish, he'd earn it all back again. The difference between Noah as an adult and Noah as a homeless kid was that he was no longer helpless. He had control over his life, and he could make his destiny what he wanted it to be.

He refused to believe anything else.

"Hey, man, sorry I'm late."

Noah turned toward the voice and saw his friend Tyson pulling out the chair next to his and sitting down.

"You're just in time," he said as the curtains were drawn and a single spotlight appeared on the stage, highlighting a woman dressed in what looked like a skimpy arrangement of black scarves and silver spangles.

Once his gaze had traveled up the flawless expanse of torso and over the lush curves of breasts, Noah realized it was Arianna Day standing in the spotlight, poised to begin dancing, her arms overhead, her face cast to the side, her hair in a complicated pile of marabou feathers and brown curls.

A heavy beat, combined with the sound of a sitar, filled the air. Then her hips began gyrating, slowly at first, then faster and faster, until she was moving double-time to the beat.

And Noah felt as if his body was catching fire as he watched. He shifted uncomfortably in his seat.

"Damn," Tyson muttered, his gaze fixed on Arianna. "That's one fine-looking honey."

"Yeah, I guess." Noah had no idea why he felt the need to act casual, or why he didn't really appreciate his best friend making any observations about the beauty of a woman he had no claim on.

Tyson caught his eye and looked at him as if he was nuts. "You been dipping into your little brother's stash of the ganja?"

"No."

"'Cause you gotta be smoking something if you don't think that girl is hot."

"She's not a girl. She's the owner of this place."

"You banging her or what?"

Any other time, Noah would have taken his friend's crassness in stride, but he felt himself bristle now. "No, but I am planning to buy this business from her, and I'd like to keep sex out of the transaction, if you don't mind."

"Sure you would," Tyson said, sounding maddeningly dubious. "Tell me the last time you managed to keep sex out of it when a beautiful woman's involved."

"Go to hell."

Noah stared at Arianna, though, as she undulated across the stage, so they went silent for a few moments, allowing him to dwell on the fact that this was the second time in a week that someone close to him had implied he was all about sex when it came to women.

Well… What guy wasn't?

But when Simon had joked that he was a sex addict, Noah hadn't been able to shake the feeling that maybe his brother was right. He couldn't ignore the guilty feeling in his gut that had lingered all day.

Sex addict? Him?

Could it be true?

When he considered the past few years, he could see that he'd gone from having a fairly normal sex life to consuming women like candy, one after another. He'd become insatiable, it seemed, and he was afraid to consider why.

Was he really as bad as his brother and his friend were insinuating?

He tried to count the number of women he'd slept with in the past year, but he couldn't remember them all. Then he tried to remember the name of the woman he'd brought home last, and he couldn't remember that, either.

It was true, then. He was just as bad as they'd said.

The terrible weight of the truth settled in his gut. Sex addiction? It was the kind of thing people sought treatment for, and he wasn't the kind of person who needed a shrink.

Not like his brother. Or his mother.

Through all the trouble he'd endured for both of them, he'd always found some solace in knowing that at least he was the lucky one. Lucky enough to be the sane, balanced one in the family. But what if he wasn't at all?

All his smug assurance that he'd gotten off easy in the mental health department was just an illusion. Or so it was beginning to seem.

No, he was being ridiculous. He wasn't crazy. He was a red-blooded male who loved women and sex. That wasn't crazy at all. It was normal.

Normal, damn it. One hundred percent.

THE FINAL ACT OF the show involved all three dancers in the troupe. All beautiful women and talented artists, but Arianna stood out as by far the best of the four. It wasn't hard to see why she drew crowds to her performances.

Noah didn't touch his food when she was onstage. It had only been between her acts that he'd managed to finish his steak and have a somewhat tense conversation with Tyson.

He didn't like the truth about himself that had been thrust upon him, even inadvertently, by his friend. And it had put him in a terrible mood. Soon he'd have to rouse himself enough to meet with Arianna and deal with whatever nuttiness she wanted to introduce into their business deal.

As the dancers took their final bows and the crowd stood

and clapped to show their appreciation, Tyson offered a half-hearted round of applause as he stifled a yawn.

Once the noise died down enough for him to be heard, he said, "Hey, man, thanks for the invite. I've got an early meeting, so I'm gonna cut out of here."

"Sure, I'll catch you at the gym Saturday," Noah said, distracted as he watched the curtains close and Arianna disappear from sight.

After Tyson left, Noah sat again to finish his drink and wait. Arianna had said that she'd meet him after the show, but she hadn't mentioned where they would meet. He could only assume she'd find out from the hostess where he'd been seated and come find him, but he didn't like the idea of sitting around waiting. It put her in the position of power. So he drained the last of the scotch from his glass, placed a generous tip on the table and stood to go find Arianna.

Before he could do so, though, he heard from behind him, "Noah Kellerman?"

He turned to find Arianna. She still wore the outfit she'd performed in, which he could only assume was a calculated effort on her part to distract him. It was working.

He forced his gaze to her face. "Yes?"

She faltered, apparently confused by his familiarity. Would she recognize him as the guy she'd mistaken for a water filter salesman a few days ago?

She must have, judging by the way her face paled as she took in the sight of him.

Excellent. He had the advantage now. She was off balance, probably feeling guilty for how rude she'd been to him before, and she wasn't as likely to drive a hard bargain if he had guilt on his side.

"I'm Arianna Day, the owner of Cabaret," she said tentatively.

"Yes, I believe you'll remember we've met when you accused me of trying to sell you a water filtration system," he said evenly, as he prepared to savor watching her squirm.

But to his surprise, she didn't squirm at all. She seemed to brighten, even, at the news that she'd been rude to him. It was as if something else entirely had caused her initial tentativeness.

Instantly, a spark came into her eyes, and she smiled a slow, sensual smile as she held out her hand. "It's a pleasure to meet you again, Noah."

He took her hand in his and was surprised by the firmness of her grip. Then he recalled how upon their first meeting, she'd refused to shake his hand. Now, she held it a moment longer than necessary, letting her fingers slip from his in a way that managed to be sexy. He was surprised at how strongly his body responded to such a minor touch.

Intrigued but still wary, he followed Arianna through the restaurant—as she smiled and nodded at fans—to the back and down a hallway, where she opened a door and let him into an office.

"Have a seat," she said, gesturing to a chair.

He didn't want to let her control the situation, but he had little choice of places to sit in the small room, so he took a chair and looked around.

"Thank you for agreeing to meet me," she said as she sat opposite him behind the desk. "I hope you enjoyed the show."

"I did," he was surprised to hear himself saying. He hadn't intended to, but he'd honestly enjoyed it. "It's not my usual taste, but you're a very talented dancer."

Her mouth settled into a little Mona Lisa smile, and she simply stared at him for a moment. "I know it's not the custom to meet like this regarding selling a business, but

Cabaret is very special to me, so I hope you'll take the time to consider my request."

"I'm listening," he said evenly.

"For personal reasons, I can no longer run the business, but I feel that I owe it to the people who depend on me to make sure they have a place to work, at least for an interim period while they look for other jobs."

Noah shrugged. "They can draw unemployment. That's what it's for."

Arianna shook her head. "It doesn't pay enough to survive in this city. I can't do that to them. And we function like a family here. We take care of each other. We're friends as well as coworkers."

"That's all well and good, but—"

"Please let me finish."

She paused, letting silence settle between them. Noah realized too late that this was a bit of a power play on her part, too. She was good, he had to admit.

"It is my hope," she finally said when she was sure she had his attention, "that I can sell Cabaret to someone who respects what we've created here, and what it means to its employees and to the community that has come to love and support this place."

Noah wanted to protest, but something stopped him short. Something, as in, she'd touched a nerve.

When she'd said the place was like a family, he understood exactly why she didn't want to let him destroy it. He'd spent his whole life protecting his small, dysfunctional family, and he was more familiar with the instinct to do so perhaps than any other.

So he remained silent.

"Cabaret has become a part of this neighborhood's personality—some even claim the whole city's personality—and I feel like I would be failing many people if I didn't fight for it to remain much as it is today with the next owner."

As she watched him from across the desk, she began removing feathers and pins from her hair, and her long, dark waves cascaded over her shoulders. Her gray eyes seemed to see some part of him that he didn't want her to see, and he shifted in his seat.

Then he realized that he was aroused by her. Again.

She slowly licked her lips, and he knew then that she was playing him for all she was worth. And it was working.

"I understand your concern," he said, sounding not quite in control.

"Good," she said quietly, her voice almost a caress.

"What, exactly, are you proposing?"

"For the first six months under your ownership, I'd like you to agree not to change Cabaret in any significant way, keep all current employees unless there is some cause to fire them and allow me to act as a consultant as you transition into running the business."

Noah blinked in surprise. Her counteroffer, rather than being less restrictive than the original terms of the sale, was actually more so. This woman had balls to spare.

But he couldn't get past what she'd said—that they were a family. And she wasn't being unreasonable. She was simply trying to protect the people she cared for. That, he got.

That, he couldn't argue with.

"And after the first six months?"

"I'll leave you alone, and you can do whatever you want with the place. If you aren't convinced by then that it's worth keeping as is, you can fire everyone, reinvent the business, do whatever you want."

He considered her words, but before he could speak, she

continued, standing and rounding the desk, planting herself on the edge of it, far too close to him with her jangling scarves and her soft, round hips.

"I've poured my heart and soul into Cabaret. I just want you to take some time to get to know it, get to know the employees, see all the performers, before you decide to close it down."

If he'd been relying on everything he'd ever learned about negotiating, at that moment he would have said no, stood and walked away.

But there she was, only inches from him. He could smell her perfume, the scent of jasmine mingled with something musky and warm. He could imagine sliding his hand up her thigh, laying her back on the desk, ripping that skimpy top off her and sliding into her right there. He'd spread her legs wide, fill her up and pump himself into her until she was gasping and weak with desire.

He could almost taste her, almost touch her. And before he could clear his head to think business, he heard himself say, "Okay, you have a deal."

4

ARI COULD HARDLY wrap her mind around the fact that she'd just agreed to sell Cabaret to Sir Sex-a-Lot.

Crazy, but true. He wasn't a water purification salesman—he was a restaurateur with more cash than he knew what to do with, apparently.

The truth had spun round and round in her head as she'd talked to him. She'd wrapped up the meeting with him in a stunned daze, then left the restaurant in a hurry and gone straight home, desperate to get some time alone to process this new set of facts.

What kind of cruel joke was the universe playing on her?

That's what Arianna asked herself as she stumbled up the four flights of stairs to her apartment. She locked the door, didn't bother to turn on any lights and went straight to the window, where she opened the blinds and stared across at the window in question.

It was dark, which meant that either he wasn't home or that he was already in bed. She went to find her binoculars, then sat on the couch to wait. A few minutes later, just as she'd feared—or hoped?—the light in his living room switched on, and she spied him walking across the room, pausing in front of a table to put something down. She raised her binoculars to peer through them.

There he was, Sir Sex-a-Lot.

Except now she knew his real name, Noah Kellerman.

Looking at him now, as opposed to before when she'd never met him face-to-face, felt a lot more like sleazy voyeuristic behavior than it ever had before. She was violating his privacy.

A weird buzzing sensation rose up from her belly and took over her head, so that she couldn't form a coherent thought. She watched him through the binoculars for a few minutes more, until she couldn't stand it anymore. Now she knew the man she was watching, and he knew her. And didn't that take away the thrill.

Then Noah looked up from his mail, and it was as if he was looking right at her.

She dropped the binoculars onto the sofa and shrank into the shadows, then ducked out of the room as quickly as she could. She was pretty sure he couldn't see her when her apartment was dark and his was light, but the sensation of him looking in her direction left her feeling vulnerable, even violated. Which was ridiculous given how she was the one who'd been holding the binoculars.

In the past two years, she'd become obsessed with protecting her personal space, both her body and her apartment. She rarely had people over anymore, and she kept the curtains closed at night. She didn't want anyone to see in. Nor did she let anyone touch her if she could help it. She tried not to flinch away from a friendly pat or hug, but it was an effort, and her friends were often confused by her stiffness.

Arianna's whole life, growing up with her single mom in the city, her body had been the one thing she could trust. Her father had mostly been absent other than expensive guilt gifts he sent at birthdays and Christmas, and the occasional extravagant vacation he'd taken her on. Her mother had been an alcoholic, so confused by her sexuality for so long, by the time she'd admitted to the world that she was a lesbian, she'd already destroyed Ari's trust in her.

Her mother had been a dancer, too—had even operated a dance school for a while in the studio space Ari intended to use. Despite their shared interests, their relationship had been permanently scarred by Vivienne's drinking and self-doubt. When her mother had moved to Paris five years ago to live with her lover, it had been almost a relief. Ari didn't really miss her.

Just like always, she'd found peace within herself—in the confident grace of her body. She simply had to visualize herself completing a dance routine, and her body would successfully navigate the job for her. She had always reveled in its physicality, loved the strong, easy way her body experienced and moved through the world, and took great pleasure in its sensuality.

She went into the bedroom and drew her curtains closed, then turned on a light and began undressing. She caught a glimpse of herself in the mirror, but looked away.

Something about looking at her own naked body scared her a little now. She used to enjoy looking at herself and being looked at, but not so much anymore.

She'd once believed that without an audience, there wasn't much reason to perform. At least now she could appreciate performing regardless of who watched, but she was worried that her heart wasn't in it. Maybe having her body violated rendered her forever unable to enjoy using it the way it was intended.

No.

That was victim-thinking, and she wasn't a victim.

She wasn't going to let one ugly event ruin her career, or her whole life.

She wasn't going to be bitter anymore. She was ready to move on.

Arianna forced herself to stand in front of the mirror on the back of the bathroom door and take a good long look at her body.

Her body.

Not her audience's, not her former lovers', not her rapist's, not anyone else's.

It was hers only to use and enjoy. Only she could love it and care for it and take pleasure in it. This was the mantra her spiritual teacher, Satya, had given Ari to repeat when she felt herself slipping into feelings of negativity.

She'd always been tall and lean, with slightly exaggerated curves. Since turning thirty, her body had begun to lose the softness of youth and had taken on more angles, more of a sinewy appearance.

She trailed her fingers across the expanse of her belly and over the tattoo of cherry blossoms that wove its way across her lower abdomen. This was supposed to be her sexual peak, wasn't it? Wasn't this the time in her life when she was mature enough, experienced enough and easily aroused enough to be having the best sex ever?

Instead, she wasn't having any sex at all, except with herself.

She'd never gone for so long as an adult without having a lover, and she was beginning to feel a sense of frustration like she'd never known before.

Her thoughts returned to Noah Kellerman. She closed her eyes for a moment, and she could picture how he looked making love to a woman—strong, primal, determined. She opened her eyes again before the thoughts forced her to relieve her own sexual tension.

She went to the altar that she kept in the far corner of her bedroom. It didn't represent any specific faith, but rather encompassed bits and pieces of what felt sacred to her personally. There was a serene-looking Thai figurine of the Buddha, his gentle expression reminding her to be always calm, placid, peaceful. Next to the Buddha stood an African goddess totem carved from wood, and next to it, a framed photo of Satya, the Indian woman who'd served as her guru for the past five years.

Arianna lit a candle and a stick of incense. She went to the closet and took out her white silk robe, put it on, then sat in the lotus position on the meditation pillow in front of the altar.

The strong, spicy scent of the incense created a Pavlovian response in her when she was preparing to meditate. It told her brain that it was time to calm down and shut up. She inhaled deeply and exhaled slowly, focusing on her breath.

Moments like this, when she was so wound up it didn't seem possible for her to settle her mind enough to meditate for longer than a minute, were exactly when she needed to do it most. Meditation had saved her life, kept her sane and soothed her in recent years.

She closed her eyes and tried to clear her mind of thoughts, paying attention only to her breathing. In, out, in, out…

She willed the tension from her shoulders, her neck and her arms. Focusing part by part, she forced her muscles to relax.

And her mind, fighting her every moment, was not easy to keep quiet. A thought crept in—Noah. What if he'd ever seen her watching him? And what if he found out where she lived and put two and two together?

No, stop it. No worrisome thoughts. Not right now.

But…

Just breathe.

In…out…in…out.

Her shoulders were tense again, so she concentrated on relaxing them.

But what if Noah...

Stop it!

Back to focusing on her breathing.

And soon a wondrous thing happened. She found it, the space she'd been struggling to reach—a quiet place in her head to dwell.

In that place, she had no sense of the passage of time or the state of her body. It had taken her several years of daily practice before she'd learned to get there so quickly, and even still, she had days when it was impossible to reach.

But she was there now.

Her mind blank, a sense of euphoria that was greater even than the way she felt onstage overcame her, then a truth came to her, fully formed, and illuminated the way a revelation occasionally arrived in her mind after meditating.

In her mind's eye she saw Noah Kellerman, and her treacherous body hummed with excitement.

She wanted him. She really and truly wanted a man again.

Wanted a lover.

Wanted Noah.

Her body warmed with each passing moment, until it was all she could do not to slide her fingers between her legs and attempt to ease the aching desire that hummed there.

She opened her eyes again, and her gaze landed on the wrinkled brown face of Satya. A year ago, Ari had traveled to India to visit her guru's ashram. The old woman had looked into Ari's eyes, seeing right through her, and proclaimed she was burning up with desire, that she wouldn't be able to put out the fire until she faced her own personal truths.

That sentiment had meant very little to her at the time.

She'd meditated on it for months, tried to make sense of it, but understanding eluded her. Until tonight.

Only now did she grasp exactly how she was burning up with desire.

And here was one of her personal truths, finally arriving to light her path.

Perhaps taking Noah Kellerman as a lover would clear her mind enough to figure out a few more truths.

The moment that thought formed in her head, she knew she would do it. Or at least she'd try. And judging by how easily he'd responded to her tonight, on top of how willingly he seemed to take new lovers himself, she didn't have any reason to believe her efforts would fail.

Noah, the only man she ever fantasized about anymore, was going to be the one to end her two-year exile from her own sexuality. When the student was ready, the teacher appeared, right?

So that must have been why he'd shown up in her life, wanting to buy Cabaret. This was her sign from the universe that it was time to reclaim herself.

With that revelation, her body hummed like a tuning fork. She stood, shrugged off the robe, blew out the candle and went to bed. A few moments later, she closed her eyes, thought of Noah, slid her fingers between her legs and did her best to coax the humming out long enough to get a decent night's sleep.

SIMON HAD BEEN PAINTING long enough to know that the vision in his head would not necessarily match what formed on the canvas, especially if he was working with a live subject. And that's what he was doing this time.

He sat near the window, but not in full view of it, because

he hated the idea of a hundred eyes watching him as he worked. He could hardly paint with any eyes watching him, let alone a hundred—or however many of them might be staring out from the building across the street.

He couldn't understand why his brother paid so much money to live in a fishbowl. Sure there was a good view of the city, the Golden Gate Bridge and the San Francisco Bay, but everyone else in the upper floors across the way also had a perfect view into the apartment.

The woman he was watching couldn't see him, because she was busy dancing in front of a mirror in her bedroom. He'd watched her before, and one day a few weeks ago, he'd gotten the urge to paint her. Aside from the fact that she was gorgeous, something about the way she moved was totally mesmerizing. She was doing some kind of belly dance and her hips, the way they gyrated, nearly put him in a trance.

She made him want to capture movement and life and fire in a painting.

It had been years since he'd taken a life-drawing class and learned to render with artful accuracy the lines and details of the human body. The hands and faces were the hardest to reproduce. Faces because the slightest mistake, the slightest variation from reality, would render the portrait imperfect. And yet at the same time, the face was an ever-changing subject, full of nuance, even for a subject sitting absolutely still.

Hands were a whole other problem. Simon had his theories about why, though he wouldn't be caught dead speaking them aloud. Hands, he thought, were where human intention became human deed. They expressed the soul's desires.

And that was all way too flowery and esoteric to be explaining to anyone.

He thought, though, if he tried to explain it to the dancer

across the way, she might get it. She'd understand, and she wouldn't laugh. The way she moved said so much—that she had depth, that she knew there was more going on than surface B.S.

It wasn't like he was perving on her. He could hardly look away. The only thing that made him do so was his effort to capture the image hanging around his head on canvas.

And this image, it wasn't anything like his usual style. Simon rarely veered from the small, angry, black-and-white drawings and paintings he liked to imagine were the truest representation of his artistic vision. This woman, however, required big, lush strokes, shades of red, orange and pink and a large canvas. He'd stretched this one himself to be five feet tall and four feet wide. The only place he could hide it was under the guest-room bed.

For the first time since his mother had died, he found himself painting something that was outside his comfort zone.

As an artist, he should have loved that. But it scared the hell out of him. And he'd die, too, if anyone saw this piece. He'd even gone so far as to chain-lock the door so his brother couldn't walk in and catch him painting this big monstrosity. If Noah tried to open the door, the chain would buy Simon time to hide the canvas.

Why his mother's death had made his art become even darker, Simon only partly understood. He'd been oddly re-lieved at her funeral. It was as if the dark cloud of her life's troubles had lifted, and he'd been able to see clear skies for a day. But there was no escaping that his mother's problems were his own. He'd inherited her best and worst traits, and lately, as his bipolar symptoms became more unpredictable and less responsive to medication, he'd been feeling as if she'd come back to haunt him.

Except when he watched the dancer across the way and painted in broad, crazy strokes of red and orange. She didn't practice in front of the mirror this way every day. But when she did, he was here, imprinting her movements on his gray matter, applying color to canvas. More than once, he'd brought out the painting to work on it from memory. Getting lost in the process, he felt something that could only be described as pure joy. Too bad it deserted him the second he let go of his brush.

He looked out the window again. The dancer had stopped and was simply standing in front of the mirror now, regarding herself. Her long, dark, wavy hair hung free down her back, and the flowing hot-pink skirt she wore looked as if it had been imported from India or whatever country people liked to put lots of gold and bangles on their clothes. He couldn't see any more details than that, so his mind filled in the rest.

He imagined her to be as beautiful up close as she appeared far away. She'd have dark eyes shaped like a cat's. And in them, he'd find answers to his questions. Total cornball, but that's the sense he picked up from her.

And the way she moved, she had to have danced professionally on a stage, for countless eyes to watch.

Sort of the opposite artistry from his. He performed for no one. She performed for a crowd. At least in his story she did.

Someday, he was going to figure out which apartment she lived in and give this painting to her if she wanted it.

And he'd thank her for being one of the most beautiful things he'd ever seen. Thank her for making him feel this part of himself that he'd never really felt before.

5

"So, I'VE READ OVER the contract, and it looks good to me," Cara said as she sat across the desk from Ari in the office of Cabaret.

"My terms are included?" Ari asked.

Cara nodded. "In the terms you agreed to verbally," she said in her confident deal-maker voice, "you'll act as consultant to the business for the first six months under Noah's ownership so long as there aren't any significant conflicts, and he will agree not to fire any employees without due cause or change the restaurant in any profound way."

"That sounds right." Sort of. Cara had rushed through it all so fast, Ari had trouble keeping up.

But here was the contract, all drawn up and ready. She was moments away from being free, and that idea had her so giddy she could hardly stand it.

"Good," Cara said. "Then sign here, and here, and here…"

Ari's eyes began to blur as Cara flipped through page after page of the document.

This was it. Ari had thought she'd feel scared or sad or something, when it came down to actually giving up Cabaret. But all she felt was giddy and relieved. She picked up a pen from her desk and started signing where Cara indicated. Then it was done.

She stared at the stack of documents.

She really was free.

"Congratulations," Cara said. "Are you happy?"

Her friend was staring at her as if she was afraid Ari would realize she was making the biggest mistake of her life and change her mind.

Ari laughed. "I am," she said. "I'm thrilled."

"I'll drop the papers off with Noah's agent this afternoon. Want to go have a celebratory drink?"

"How about we have one here where I have a bit of an in with the bartender? He might even hook us up with some free drinks."

"Good thinking," Cara said as she tucked the papers into her briefcase.

They left the office and walked down the hallway to the restaurant entrance. It was midafternoon, and on stage directly ahead, the red velvet stage curtains were closed. Behind another door the kitchen was beginning to bustle with activity as workers prepared for the evening. No one was staffing the bar at the moment, so Ari went behind it and played bartender.

"What'll it be, pretty lady?"

Cara gave the matter serious consideration. "Oh, I remember back in the day you could make a mean martini. Still remember how?"

"But of course." Ari set about making drinks, and as she worked, it struck her that this technically wasn't her bar anymore—or her alcohol, either.

Oh, well, surely Noah wouldn't mind them having a drink on him.

Noah Kellerman, aka Sir Sex-a-Lot.

The idea of his really owning this entire space struck her as irrefutable reality, and she stopped in her tracks.

Wow, she'd really gone and done it. She'd sold her club to the star of her sexual fantasies.

When she turned back to Cara, she must have looked stricken.

"What is it?" Cara asked.

"Can I tell you something completely bizarre?"

"I'd hate it if you didn't."

"Noah? The guy who's buying—I mean, who just bought—this place? I know him from somewhere else."

Cara's eyes widened. "Really? Where?"

Ari said nothing as she found and opened a jar of olives. She popped an olive in each glass, then slid Cara's drink across the bar to her.

She lifted her own glass. "To new beginnings," Ari said.

They clinked their glasses together, then she took a sip of her drink.

Cara watched her carefully. "Well?" she finally said when Ari didn't continue.

She glanced around to make sure no one in the vicinity was listening.

"He's my across-the-way neighbor," she said.

"He lives in the building across from yours? So you see him on the street and stuff?"

"It's way better than that."

Cara's eyes lit up with dawning recognition now. "Wait. He's not—"

"Oh, yes he *is*."

"That guy in the window? Sir Sex-a-Lot?"

Ari nodded.

"You just sold Cabaret to *Sir Sex-a-Lot?*"

Maybe six months ago, Cara had been over for dinner just in time for one of Noah's window sex fests. She and Ari had watched the spectacle over glasses of red wine and howled with laughter at the audacity—and longevity—of the whole thing.

"Yep."

"Oh. My. God."

"Crazy, I know."

"He's so good-looking up close, but I'm not going to be able to look at him without laughing."

"Tell me about it."

"Wait a minute. You've already had to face him knowing he's your exhibitionist neighbor!"

"Yep."

"Oh my God," Cara said again, then stared some more with her mouth agape.

"I know, it's crazy."

"Do you suppose he's a sex addict or something?"

"Seems kind of likely, don't you think?"

If he was, then it would be all that much easier to make him the man who ended Ari's drought.

"How many different women does he bring home?"

"I've lost count."

"And he always does it right there in the window for the whole world to see?"

"Far as I can tell. But who knows? He could be doing it on the Muni and in the alley and anywhere else he can find, for all we know."

"Wow. Just…wow." Cara shook her head and took another sip.

Footsteps caught Ari's attention, and she turned to see the bartender, Kip, approaching with an eager expression on his face.

"I couldn't help but overhear," he said. "You sold Cabaret to a sex addict? Delicious."

Oh, dear God. Kip was the world's worst gossip. Or at least

the worst of any of her employees. Being a bartender gave him an endless supply of info to dish.

She gave him the evil eye. "You were eavesdropping."

He flashed a not-very-chagrinned expression. "I paused around the corner to tie my shoe, and maybe I stayed there a bit longer than necessary once I heard the conversation was such a juicy one."

"You can't tell anyone about this, okay?"

"Let's see—the new boss is a freak? No, I can't tell a soul. No one would care, anyway." He sounded wholly unconvincing.

Under Ari's suspicious gaze, he busied himself picking a piece of lint from his black T-shirt.

"Why don't I believe you?"

"Oh, lighten up," he said with a dismissive wave, before he slid onto a stool next to Cara and propped his elbows on the bar. "I want to hear the whole scoop."

"There is no scoop. You just heard everything I know."

"So he has sex in front of his window, for the whole neighborhood to watch?"

"I'm not talking about it to you."

"C'mon, if you don't set me straight, you know I'll spread inaccurate facts that are probably way worse than the truth."

"Like when you told everyone I was a lesbian?"

"Well, that wasn't worse than the truth—it was better. No one wanted to hear that you're simply boring and frigid."

"Shut up." Ari rolled her eyes and pulled a bottle of Corona out of the fridge for Kip. She popped the cap, topped the bottle with a wedge of lime and presented him with what she hoped would be an adequate bribe. Despite his propensity for salacious news, she did count him as a friend. Talking too much was pretty much his only bad quality.

He was one of the only people at Cabaret who knew she hadn't gotten laid in two years, though he didn't know why. The lesbian-but-not-out-of-the-closet rumor was his good-natured stab at the reason.

Chastened a bit, Kip poked at his lime until it slid down the neck of the bottle and into the beer.

"So how much do you hate Ari for selling this place?" Cara asked.

"Oh, tons. I mean, how could she?"

Cara smiled a slightly tipsy smile—she was a cheap date, and her martini was gone already—and leaned in close. "I told her not to do it," she said in a stage whisper.

"I'm leaving now, if you two are going to harass me," Ari said.

She needed to start cleaning out the office, anyway.

"Don't be mad! We'll leave you alone—promise. Stay here and get drunk with us."

Ari stopped in her tracks and sighed. Cleaning out the office could wait another half hour. How many more times was she going to be able to hang out at Cabaret's bar and help herself to free drinks?

"C'mon, pour yourself another one and tell me the down and dirty on the divine Noah Kellerman," Kip said, a dreamy smile on his face.

"Do I sense a crush?" Ari asked.

"He's as straight as a board, but I can fantasize."

Truly, if Noah was going to have sex for the world to see, then what was the point of her keeping his behavior a secret? After all, if she had her way, she was going to be the next woman in his picture window.

She set about making a second round of martinis as she filled in Kip on all the lurid details.

WHEN NOAH GOT the call on his cell phone while on his way home from the gym that Arianna had signed the contract, he'd been unable to resist going straight over to Cabaret. His hair was still wet from showering at the gym, but he'd at least changed into a pair of jeans and a sweater. It was late afternoon, around the time when he'd expect to find a few employees prepping to open later, but he was surprised to see instead when he walked in, Arianna leaning against the bar talking to the bartender.

They were smiling and laughing, appearing to have a grand time. "That's ridiculous," Arianna was saying, right before she looked over and saw Noah in the doorway.

He nodded and headed toward her.

"Noah," she said, clearly shocked. "Hello."

"I got a call from my broker that you'd signed the contract, and I couldn't resist stopping in," he said.

"Oh, well, sure. I mean, of course. The place is nearly yours now, after all. I know there's escrow and all to get through, but that's only a formality, right?"

Noah nodded. "So long as Cabaret doesn't have any hidden debts, or—"

"Of course it doesn't," she said, appearing shocked at the very idea.

The bartender was watching the two of them with keen interest.

"Kip," Arianna said. "I don't think you two have been formally introduced. This is Cabaret's new owner, Noah Kellerman. Noah, this is our—I mean, um, *your*—head bartender extraordinaire, Kip Reed."

Noah had seen Kip already. He'd watched him at the bar and had admired the man's confident deftness serving drinks.

But he couldn't say he liked the smug twinkle in Kip's gaze now. As if he knew the punch line of a joke Noah hadn't heard.

"My pleasure," Kip said, extending a hand to Noah.

He had a handshake that lingered a bit too long, and Noah finally pulled his hand away, uncomfortable with the guy-on-guy contact.

"You've got good timing," Arianna said as she patted a box sitting on the bar beside her. "I was packing up my stuff in the office and wondering about some furniture that I could either leave behind or take with me."

"You work fast," Noah said. "Didn't you just sign the contract a couple of hours ago?"

She shrugged. "I was already here and I thought I might as well go ahead and move some of my things upstairs to the dance studio."

"Sure."

Arianna turned to Kip, who was busy pretending to wipe down the bar as he eavesdropped on them. "We'll be in the office if anyone needs me," she said.

Kip eyed them curiously but said nothing as Noah followed Arianna.

Today she wore street clothes for the first time since he'd met her—a flouncy purple gypsy-looking dress that hugged her torso and waist before flaring out and a pair of brown knee-high boots. The look reminded Noah of saloon girls. Did the woman ever wear a normal shirt and pair of jeans?

He'd guess not.

Once they were inside the office, she closed the door behind them. Then she locked it.

He eyed the lock, perplexed.

"Oh," she said, looking a little embarrassed. "It's second nature. Around this place, you'd better make it a habit to lock the door unless you want people barging in every other minute mistaking your office for a bathroom or a supply closet."

"Isn't there a sign on the door that says Private?"

"Yeah, and people never seem to read it. Maybe you could get a bigger sign."

Noah looked around at the office. He'd seen it before, but now he noticed how much of Arianna's personal touch it had. A burgundy feather boa was draped carelessly over the laser printer behind the desk, a pair of dangly gold earrings lay next to the lamp—which also, incidentally, was bedecked with feathers. He wasn't sure he'd ever seen so many feathers in his life as he had around Arianna.

His gaze landed on the far wall, which had been painted red. On it hung a wide rod that extended the width of the wall, and on the rod hung a curtain of crystal beads. The effect was dazzling in an obvious way, like the rest of Cabaret. He felt as if he were inside a jewelry box.

"Let me guess—not your style," Arianna said as she watched him take in the room.

He smiled and shrugged. "Crystal beaded curtains wouldn't be my first choice."

"I know we still have to get through escrow, and that'll take what? A few weeks?"

"Up to a month maybe, but I'm not sure. I'll have to ask the escrow agent."

"If you're comfortable getting yourself settled here now, I'm happy to accommodate you and start transitioning to you running the business."

Noah blinked. He hadn't expected her to offer this, and he didn't know what to make of it. If there were some problem during the escrow process that suddenly made the business undesirable, he'd be wasting his time here, but...

It didn't seem likely.

"That's very generous of you," he said. "I'll definitely give the matter some serious thought and let you know."

She nodded. "No rush. I'll be ready when you are."

"There is one favor I'd like to ask. I'm wondering if there are any open positions in the kitchen right now. My little brother needs a job."

"The dishwasher quit a week ago. Would he be willing to do that?"

"I'll see if I can get him to. Should I have him contact you?"

She waved a hand to dismiss the idea. "Of course not. If you want to hire him, he's got the job. I'm really hoping you'll consider Cabaret yours. Operational decisions—all of it."

He took a step farther into the room, looking around at the furniture, most of which appeared to be odds and ends with a distinct flea market vibe. Arianna closed the space between them, creating an awkward closeness that reminded him of the last time they were in the office together.

Either this woman had no sense of personal space, or…

Or what? She really wanted to be close to him?

The possibility certainly wasn't unpleasant to consider.

"So what do you think?" she said. "Should I clear the office out completely, or is there anything here you'd like me to leave?"

"Don't you need this stuff for your dance studio's office?"

"There's already a desk and some seating up there, but I could fit some of this stuff there if need be. Some of it I'll probably give to whomever wants to take it home, if you don't want it."

Noah nodded. "Whenever it's convenient for you, just clear the room. I'll bring in my own furniture."

He expected her to move away, but instead she simply stared at him, a Cheshire cat smile playing on her lips.

"What's so funny?" he said, reminded now of Kip and his mysterious amusement.

"It's just…" Her gaze dropped to his mouth. "I'm still feeling a little ridiculous for mistaking you for a salesman the first time you came to Cabaret."

He got the distinct feeling that wasn't what she'd been smiling about at all. He'd been flirted with by enough women to know what her body language—hips slightly forward, too close to him, chin upturned, gaze half-lidded—meant.

She wanted him.

And under any other circumstances, that would have been a lucky fact indeed. But now?

Sex addict.

The words popped into his head at odd times. While playing basketball at the gym, while showering, while trying to fall asleep last night.

He didn't want to feel as screwed up in the head as his brother or his mother had been. He had to prove to himself that his being a sex addict was an empty accusation, that it didn't carry the ring of truth.

But that meant not having sex, didn't it?

"Don't give it another thought," he said. "I haven't."

He took a step back and found his calf bumping against the sofa behind him. A step to the side, and he had a bit of breathing space.

Arianna still looked amused.

"So will this be your first restaurant venture?"

"Actually, my third. The first two I opened in L.A."

"I'd love to hear about them," she said as he turned and examined a collage of photos on the wall.

They were mostly shots of people at Cabaret. The restaurant, bar and kitchen served as a backdrop for smiling groups of people. His gaze landed on a shot of Arianna in costume, standing with two other costumed women he recognized from her dance troupe. She wore heavy makeup, her hair up in a coil of braids and beads. A skimpy silver coin bra barely contained her ample breasts, and her bare torso was accented by an elegant floral tattoo near her left hip that disappeared at the waist of a mostly see-through skirt.

He couldn't look away, and he couldn't stop imagining what it would feel like to have her beneath him, to be inside her hot, wet—

Stop it.

She'd just said something to him…. But he couldn't remember what they'd been talking about seconds ago.

She was at his elbow now. He could smell the warm cotton-candy scent of her.

"This is my Cabaret wall—pictures from my time here. Once I started it, people kept giving me more and more photos to put up. It's been a great run," she said, sounding wistful.

He pointed to a photo of her standing behind the bar holding a bottle of vodka. "You look different there somehow."

"Oh God, that was years ago. I was still a baby."

Noah studied the photo more closely. "It's not that you look so much younger. It's more like…some quality in your eyes. You look kind of innocent, I guess."

She snorted. "Yeah, that's one way to put it."

Noah looked at her, surprised by the sudden sarcasm in her tone. "Does that mean you're cynical and bitter now?"

She smiled. "Isn't that what life does to people?"

The sarcasm was gone, as quickly as it had appeared.

"I suppose, but you don't strike me as a cynical person."

"You don't know me yet."

Yet.

He didn't like how thrilled he was by the idea of getting to know her. Especially not when his method of getting to know women typically involved no more than five dates and a strict let's-keep-this-about-sex policy.

And yet, it was impossible to separate sex and Arianna. She exuded her sexuality in a way that was hard not to notice. There was something he couldn't put his finger on, though—almost like a wall behind her flirtatious gaze, as if she were inviting him close, but not too close.

"Looks like you've got a lot of great memories from this place," he said.

"Like I told you, this is my family. I'll really miss that part of running Cabaret."

"You'll be right upstairs. You can always come down to visit."

"It's not the same. Working hard together on a slammed night, sitting around bored together on an empty night, joking about awful customers—that's the kind of thing I'll miss."

Noah had never allowed himself to get close to his staff at previous restaurants. He'd kept himself separate, mostly out of necessity because he didn't have the time or desire to cultivate friendships with his employees. Through Arianna he got a glimpse of what he might have been missing out on.

His own family had never looked so happy as this haphazard one on the wall did. He didn't even have many family photos—a few of his mom from her own childhood that she'd hung on to over the years. That was it.

Noah turned to Arianna and found her standing closer than he'd expected again. This time, though, she tilted her chin up to him, a challenge. Her gaze said, *I dare you.*

It was unmistakable what she wanted.

So that was how she wanted to play it.

He clenched his jaw and glanced over her head, wondering if he had the willpower to bolt.

But the look she gave him started a warming sensation in his chest that shot straight to his groin. His cock stirred, and he knew he wasn't going to get out of the room blameless.

Maybe he was an addict. And she was his crack cocaine.

"Noah," she said, her voice a low, silky purr.

And without saying another word, he knew what she meant: let's don't fight this.

So he didn't. He slid his hand around her waist and kissed her.

6

ARI'S FIRST KISS in more than two years, and she was thrilled to see she hadn't forgotten how to do it.

Not that Noah would have noticed any tentativeness if she had. He didn't just kiss her—he consumed her. Before she knew it, he'd lifted her off her feet as his tongue searched out hers and his lips coaxed her further and further into the kiss.

Given his earlier standoffishness, she was surprised how easily he'd taken her cues a moment ago.

And surprised how easily this was all coming to her. She'd spent two years recoiling from any man's touch. So how was it that soon as this man reached out and pulled her to him, it felt like slipping into a dance routine she'd been practicing her entire life?

When the student is ready, the teacher appears.

Was she ever ready. Satya's wise, timeless face appeared in Ari's mind's eye for a moment, smiling her approval, and a surge of pure joy washed through Ari.

Noah's hands were all over her, pulling her back to the present with their searching and coaxing and grasping. She could hardly believe how hard and solid he felt against her, or how delicious his mouth tasted, or how the musky scent of him was so completely intoxicating she was sure she'd fall into a swoon if he let go of her now.

He pushed up her dress and found his way beneath it, his fingers grazing her bare torso, then finding her breasts, then teasing and coaxing her nipples until they couldn't get any more erect. He trailed his lips down her neck over her chest, then to her breasts.

He first tasted her through the black lace of her bra but quickly grew impatient and tugged the bra down, as Arianna pulled her dress off and tossed it aside. Now she wore only her half-removed bra, panties and boots. She marveled at the feel of being naked with a man again.

A man.

This was how it was supposed to feel. And with that thought, tears pricked at her eyes. She closed them and brought her thoughts back to that very moment—Noah's mouth sucking her breast. The delicious tugging went straight to her core, and she could not have stopped Noah any more than she could have halted a speeding train.

She frantically unfastened his pants and found his erection straining against a pair of blue boxer briefs. She gripped his cock and savored its heat and firmness, so foreign to her. She had no fear or doubt—she wanted him inside her.

Needed him inside her.

Now.

She grabbed him by the hair and tugged him up to face her. "I want you," she said, her voice little more than a gasp.

There was no way he could doubt her meaning, but just to make sure he didn't, she slid her hand inside his briefs and palmed the hot flesh of his erection. A low groan escaped his throat.

The look he gave her was pure hunger. She'd seen it before, through her binoculars. And now here she was, living out her fantasy, everything so much more real and tactile than what her imagination could produce.

"Here?" he said, looking for the briefest moment doubtful.

"Now," she said as she began tugging his shirt over his head.

He pulled it the rest of the way off, then took off her bra and tugged down her panties, leaving her only in the boots, and she was relieved to see that she didn't care at all. This physical intimacy, it felt…really good.

"This is crazy," he said, breathless as he took off his shoes and pants. He was here in her office, only inches away. He got out his wallet and removed a condom, and Ari's mouth went dry.

This was really happening. And she wasn't going to let fear take hold of her for even a moment. Instead, she pushed up off the edge of the desk where she'd been leaning and took the package from his hand.

She tore it open and slid the condom over his cock, pausing to let her fingertips graze his balls, feeling them tighten against her touch.

He exhaled noisily and grabbed her, pulled her over to the couch, covered his body with hers. Then they were kissing in a desperate frenzy, and her legs were around his hips, and she could feel him pressing into her…almost there, almost, pushing against the natural resistance of her body…

One firm thrust, and he was inside her. *He was inside her.* How had she denied herself this pleasure for so long? This sensation of her body taking him in seemed like everything she'd ever wanted or needed.

Some deep place she couldn't reach—hadn't even realized needed reaching—felt satisfied for the first time she could remember, and as he began pushing deeper into her, again and again, the delicious friction between their bodies was pure sweet agony.

She ached for more, even as he gave it to her, and the sheer strength of his muscles against her gave her something to cling to as she lost herself in the sensations of their lovemaking. They were a tangle of limbs and touches and moans, and she couldn't stop soaking it all in, as if she were a visitor to a strange new country.

Noah paused, covering her mouth in a deep, hungry kiss, then he sat back on the couch while lifting her with him, so that she straddled his lap. He slid into her easily now, where she was slippery and wet.

And as she began moving on him, her clit rubbing against his body, she felt herself dangerously close to the edge. Another movement, and another, and she'd be…

Yes. *There.*

Forgetting about prying ears that might be right outside in the hallway, she cried out, surprising herself with the energy of it, tossing her head back as an orgasm the likes of which she'd never felt before quaked through her, leaving her finally gasping and spent against Noah's shoulder.

He kissed her gently on the neck as he stroked her back. Then, once she'd recovered, he grasped her hips, lifting her slightly as he began pumping hard into her, furious with determination until moments later he, too, was overcome by his release. He gasped and pulled her hard against him, burying his face in her hair to muffle the sound of his orgasm.

Quiet and stillness overtook them, and they sat for a few long moments, tangled together.

Slowly, Ari felt herself coming back to reality. She'd done it. She'd really done it. Her long, lonely drought was over, and she'd lived out a cherished fantasy.

But now what?

She hadn't thought beyond this point. The goal had seemed

so big and insurmountable…a mountain on the horizon after a long journey. Once on the other side of it, what had she found?

She wasn't ready to consider the landscape. Instead, she untangled herself from Noah's grasp, easing off him, expelling one last ragged sigh before she dressed.

He stood and disposed of the condom in a garbage can next to the desk, then thoughtfully covered it with a piece of paper, before retrieving his own clothes from the floor.

"Well," he finally said, breaking the awkward silence. "I wasn't expecting that to happen."

She smiled. "I was."

"Guess I'm a little slow on the uptake."

"I'm not sure we'd have been able to get much accomplished together without doing something about all that sexual tension," she said, though she knew it was just an excuse.

What else was there to say? That she'd been watching him for years and had determined to screw his brains out for her own therapeutic purposes?

Not likely.

"I'd like to think this won't adversely affect our working relationship," he said.

She shrugged as she straightened out her dress. "We're both grown-ups, right?"

"Definitely grown-ups."

When she looked him in the eyes, she could see that he was a little dazed by postcoital bliss. Time to bid farewell before things got any more awkward.

"I hate to rush off," Ari said. "But I have an appointment I need to make. You're welcome to stick around here if—"

"No, that won't be necessary. I have to go, too."

Good.

"Okay, well, I'll see you soon, then—"

"I'll let you know about the escrow period," he said, heading for the door.

Perfect. He was the ultimate commitment-phobe. Something about his expression said it all. He wanted out of here fast.

She lifted her hand in a little wave as he unlocked the door and disappeared down the hallway. Her body still tingled from sex.

Sex.

She couldn't help smiling, even as something a little less comforting than happiness poked at her gut. She was back in the saddle again, and she wasn't about to let anything bring her down now.

Sex addict.

With each step he took away from Arianna's office, the words echoed in his head. As he passed the bar on his way out, Kip eyed him again, this time doing a really bad job of acting as though he wasn't curious about what had gone on in the office.

"Bye, Mr. Kellerman!" he said as Noah headed for the front door.

"It's Noah—just call me Noah," he answered. "See you later."

Outside, he realized too late that he'd hoped to take a closer look at the kitchen than he had on previous visits to see if there was any equipment he'd want to replace.

Well, he wasn't going back now.

Sex addict.

Damn it, why did Simon have to go and suggest such a stupid thing? Noah wasn't an addict. He was a guy who liked sex. Which made him just like every other guy on the planet.

But what the hell had just happened in there? Usually, he was the one who could look at a woman and know in an instant if he'd be taking her to bed. With Arianna, though, he'd intended to keep things professional. He was certainly capable of doing that—in theory, anyway—and he hadn't expected their brief perusal of the office furniture to turn into a quick-and-dirty screw on the office sofa.

And damn it, so what if it had? That wasn't a bad thing. That was a good thing—a really good thing. It was every guy's fantasy.

As he strode toward his condo, he alternately mulled over his odd mixed feelings, and savored the memories of his encounter with Arianna. God, she'd been so eager and forceful. He couldn't remember the last time a woman had turned him on so much.

Noah stepped inside the door of his condo half hoping to find himself alone, and half hoping Simon would be there. He wanted to pop open a bottle of champagne and celebrate signing the papers, but Simon was across the room painting, and Noah knew from experience that he'd only piss off his little brother by proposing he take a break.

"Hey, Simon. How's it going?"

Simon, in the middle of mixing white acrylic paint with black in what looked like an effort to achieve the perfect almost-black gray—this wasn't his first effort—didn't pause in his work or even look up. He was sitting on one of the bar stools next to the counter, his art supplies spread out on the black quartz countertop and an easel set up before him holding a blank canvas. When Noah came closer, he could see that there were actually pencil marks on it depicting the weird, claustrophobic images that were Simon's trademark.

This one was of a woman, sort of a princess figure, frolicking in a field of flowers. Nearby stood a giant oak tree. But the subject matter was completely at odds with the style and tone of the drawing. When his brother was done with it, the painting would be somewhere between haunting and downright creepy.

"A princess?" he asked, watching as Simon dabbed the first bit of gray on the figure's dress.

"Something like that."

Simon was always willfully obtuse about his art. Noah had never gotten a straight answer from him about much of anything.

"I've got some great news." Noah paused for effect, but his audience was too busy mixing paint to care.

"Yeah?" Simon said without looking up.

"My offer was accepted. The restaurant's mine."

"So you're back in business. Congrats, man," he said as if he didn't really give a damn.

"The dishwasher quit last week, so I was hoping you'd be generous enough to step in and help me out. You know, until a serving job or cook position opens up."

Again Simon said nothing. He was as creative in the kitchen as he was on canvas, and if he hadn't dropped out of culinary school after getting kicked out of art school—a feat Noah hadn't even realized was possible until his little brother accomplished it—he'd probably be working as a chef right now.

Although, that assumed Simon would be able to hold down such a job, or not cave under such responsibility, which assumed a lot.

Quite a lot.

It wasn't that he was a lousy employee or an irresponsible person on his good days. But on his rare bad days, his anxiety and anger were a bit much for most employers and at least one art school to tolerate.

"So? What do you say? Help a brother out?"

"Sure, whatever, man."

"Don't fall all over yourself thanking me or anything. I thought we should start looking for a place for you, too."

This got his attention finally. He looked up from his painting. "My own apartment?"

"I saw a studio for rent down the street from the restaurant. You could have space to do your art."

"Yeah, and I wouldn't have to vacate the premises so you can have your booty calls."

And no more dripping paint on my bamboo floors. Noah thought it better not to add that comment.

"So when can we go look at it?"

"I'll give the owner a call and find out. But we need to have a serious talk about the job thing first."

Simon expelled a put-upon sigh, and Noah resisted the urge to get offended. His brother liked to go through the motions of being a pain in the ass, but Noah knew at heart, Simon really did appreciate the help.

Or Noah was pretty sure Simon did.

They'd been closer than most brothers, thanks to the odd and scary circumstances of their upbringing. For most of his life, he'd counted Simon, different as they were, as his best friend. Most of the time, underneath all the attitude, he knew Simon felt the same.

"Go ahead, tell me how I need to make sure I don't freak out on the job, offend my fellow employees or skip work for weeks at a time."

"That's not what I was going to say."

"Then what?" Simon put down the paintbrush and gave Noah his full attention.

"I don't want this to be a dead-end job for you. If you seriously want to work your way onto the cooking staff and into a chef position, then I'm going to help you make that happen.

But if—" He paused and looked at the painting again. "If what you really want is to have time to pursue your art, then I want to see you approaching some galleries here in the city. You're good enough to get a show."

Simon's gaze darted toward the window. He'd always been insecure about his artistic talents, which had kept him from doing anything with his work.

"I don't know, man."

"Listen, you're turning thirty this year. Doesn't that scare you a little? Make you want to steer your life in a certain direction?"

Simon laughed. "Well, I hadn't really thought about it. But, now that you mention it…"

"Just think about it. Getting your own studio, a new job… Consider it a fresh start."

"What's with all the nagging?"

"I don't want you to ever look back on your life and regret not having pursued your dreams."

Simon stared at him, expressionless, for a few long moments. Then he smirked and shook his head. "Okay, bro. You win. I'll get with the program."

"Which means what?"

"I'll be a good boy washing dishes, and I'll start approaching galleries, and I'll go for a cook position when one comes open. Might as well have a backup plan in case the art thing doesn't pan out."

Noah nodded, careful not to let his relief show too much. "You want to go check the new restaurant out with me? I mean, after you finish painting?"

Simon shrugged. "Sure."

And Noah smiled. This might actually work. It really might work. Seeing his brother stable and successful in life was at least as big a dream for him as his own success had been.

He left Simon to his painting and walked across the living room to the picture window, where a black leather cushioned platform served as an oversize window seat. Before today, it had also been the site of his many conquests. One woman after another, he'd brought here, had sex with, then forgot.

Until today… Arianna wasn't the kind of woman a guy had sex with and forgot, though. She got under his skin. Stayed with him. She was quite unforgettable. In fact, despite their clear no-strings message to each other, Noah found himself plotting their next encounter. Already he had a list of dirty, sexy and very satisfying things he wanted to do to her. And didn't that beg a question?

He stared out past the buildings and rooftops at the view of the bay, which was shrouded in fog.

Was he really a sex addict?

Judging by the way he responded to Arianna and the loop of images of him and her on the desk, on the couch, running through his brain…

Like he was a junkie, and she was his drug.

There was some quality she had, some bit of vulnerability beneath her brazen exterior, that set him on alert the way no other woman ever had. Watching her reminded him of the way it felt to watch a beautiful gazelle, drinking at a stream, and knowing the lion lurked in the grass, about to pounce.

The lion was him, and he was hungry.

But he hated feeling like a predator. He'd always seen his sexual activities as relationships between equals. But this thing with Arianna, it shook him.

As did that label—*sex addict.*

He wasn't even sure he knew what it meant, so he went to his desk and brought the computer out of sleep mode. He opened up his Internet browser and typed the words *sex addiction* in the search field. He hit Enter, then scrolled through the results until he found a link to a reputable medical Web site. He clicked on it, and a moment later, he was staring at a detailed article on sexual addiction and its symptoms.

His stomach churned as he began reading. When he reached a questionnaire entitled Are You a Sex Addict?, he almost closed the browser rather than read it.

But as he scanned the list, he was relieved to see that his answers to most of the questions were no.

Did he engage in compulsive masturbation?

No.

Did he frequently view pornography?

No.

Did he solicit prostitutes?

No.

Did his sexual activities interfere with daily life?

No.

Well, mostly no.

Did his romantic relationships tend to be short-lived?

Yes.

He read on.

No, no, no, no, no, yes, no, no, no, yes, no, no.

Okay, three and a half yeses. That wasn't so bad.

Except, at the bottom of the list he read the statement:

If you answer yes to any one of these questions, consider seeking help from a mental-health professional or
a local chapter of Sex Addicts Anonymous.

Any *one* of these questions?

Feeling guilty after sexual encounters and relationship

difficulties due to sexual appetite were enough to qualify him as a sex addict?

This Web site was obviously a little alarmist. He clicked back to his search results list, scanned some more and found another sex addiction checklist.

And again, he found himself qualifying for a lifetime of sexual dysfunction counseling.

Noah sighed, rose from his seat and paced into the kitchen for a drink of water. Then he returned to the living room, and as he passed the large picture window, he stopped again and looked out at the building across the way.

How many people there had watched him get it on over the past few years? And why had he felt such an instinctive need to be watched?

Exhibitionist.

One of the questionnaires had mentioned voyeurism and exhibitionism as problems associated with sex addiction, and that label, at least, rang true, though he'd never really thought of himself that way before. It wasn't as though he was having sex in crowded train cars or on a stage.

Except, well… He looked down at the window seat and out again at the many windows that stared back at his. He tended not to look at the building next door, because it wasn't quite tall as the building he was in, and from his penthouse vantage point, he tended to look beyond it at the stunning view he was paying the premium price for.

Okay, so he was having sex on a stage for countless people to watch.

He went back to his computer and did another Google search, this time for psychologists who specialized in sexual issues in San Francisco.

Three more searches had him settled on Dr. Lily Chen,

whom several message boards had referred to as the best in the city. He wrote down her number so he could call her later, when Simon wasn't around.

Then he opened up his e-mail and saw that the interior designer he'd hired had sent him a note asking when they could get started. He'd yet to tell the designer there would be a delay, that his own restaurant concept, Door 22, was going to have to wait a bit while he went through the guise of fulfilling his ridiculous obligation to Arianna Day.

There wouldn't be a six-month delay while Cabaret continued to operate, though. Not if things worked out the way he expected. She'd signed the contract he'd had drawn up without making any changes to his wording. He suspected she and her agent hadn't read closely enough, and hadn't seen that he'd inserted a clause stating that he'd comply with the six-month period as long as there were no significant conflicts. If a conflict arose—and he'd guarantee it would—and an arbitrator couldn't solve it within a week, he was free to dismiss Arianna as consultant and change the restaurant as he saw fit.

He doubted any of it would hold up in a court of law, but he also doubted she'd bother taking him to court. This was all about her having trouble letting go of a place she loved. But he'd make sure working with him wasn't the most enjoyable experience.

And he only had to get past his attraction to her long enough to do so.

He began typing a note to the designer, asking her to hold off on the project until further notice.

"I'll be ready soon as I wash up these brushes," Simon said from across the room.

Noah imagined his mother smiling down from heaven.

He was about to set up Simon with a job and an apartment, and he was about to realize his own dream. This was it— they'd made it. He could only hope she'd be proud.

7

THE DANCE STUDIO had two walls of mirrors and a large hardwood floor that Ari had had waxed to a high shine. The place smelled new again, thanks to the wax and the fresh coat of paint.

Over the speaker system, she had a nature soundtrack playing—something called "Heart of the Jungle"—while she sat in the middle of the floor stretching her hamstring muscles. Birdsongs and monkey cries seemed a little out of place in her dance studio, but she needed something to take her mind off Noah.

Turned out, having him right downstairs, and right outside her window—though she made a point not to look at him now—was a wee bit distracting. She hadn't bargained on jonesing for him constantly.

But it had been nearly a week since they'd gotten down and dirty in her old office, and no amount of telling herself she'd only wanted a bit of sexual relief from him was convincing her heart it was true.

She wasn't sure what she wanted, except for him to get the hell out of her head. More sex, maybe. Sure, why not? Except that he'd been standoffish the few times they'd been together.

He'd stopped by Cabaret a few days later to let her know that he was willing to informally start taking over running the place. She'd been in the middle of a rush, short one bartender and serving drinks herself, and she hadn't had time to talk.

The day after that, he'd shown up ready to be debriefed about operations, and they'd gone through the motions in a completely professional manner, careful to be circumspect in front of all the employees eyeing them curiously. And it seemed as if Noah had been careful not to end up anywhere alone with her.

Yet she'd thought about him nearly nonstop.

It wasn't like he was her type. He was so clean-cut, so straitlaced and probably way more conservative than she could handle. Except for his sexual appetite, of course. And that's what kept her up at night. All that sensual intensity beneath a business-clone exterior. She found the contrast exciting somehow.

She heard a tap on the door and turned to see Noah peering at her through the glass. Speak of the devil. No surprise that the sight of him turned her insides to jelly instantly.

She waved him in.

"Hey," he said. "Sorry to interrupt. If you're busy—"

"No, not at all. I'm just doing a little postrehearsal stretching. My dance troupe left a half hour ago."

He stepped inside and looked around. "This is nice."

"How are things going downstairs?" She was surprised how easily she'd been able to leave him alone with the running of the place. After a few hours it was apparent he could handle it—perhaps better than she ever had.

"Actually that's why I'm here. I was wondering if you'd mind helping out tonight."

She stood. "You don't think that would be too many cooks in the kitchen?"

"I'm thinking the place might need an assistant manager.

I know you've been doing it all yourself, but I may not have as much stamina as you." He flashed a rueful smile.

She wasn't quite sure she believed him. She hadn't witnessed any flagging stamina. "I did have an assistant manager until about a month ago. He went off to law school, and since I was selling the place I didn't get around to hiring someone new."

"It's going to be a busy night. We've got that world music band scheduled to play—"

"Yeah, they're very popular."

"Our tables are booked solid."

"And you'll want to make sure the dance floor is cleared, because people will definitely dance."

Noah made a face. "You mean we need to move the tables?"

Ari nodded. "They all fit even when they're not overlapping the dance floor. It's just a bit crowded."

She could tell by his expression that he was none too keen on the idea of crowding his customers together. But she'd always found it created a more intimate atmosphere. People somehow started having a better time once they were packed in like sardines.

He was still standing right next to the door with his hand on the knob, as if he needed to make sure he had a fast escape route.

Ari wasn't sure whether to find this amusing or offensive. They hadn't spoken of their lovemaking since it had happened, and now she wondered. Had he been repulsed by her or something? Was there some air of rape victim she exuded that she wasn't aware of?

No, that was ridiculous. She wasn't going to take the blame for his weird behavior.

"While you're here, let me give you something," she said, walking over to the desk.

She could have brought it to him later, but she wanted to see him let go of the damn door and relax in her presence.

"I really should get back—"

"It'll just take a second."

She sat and began writing a list of names. There were at least three employees who'd make good assistant managers. If Cabaret hadn't sold quickly she'd intended to approach one of them about the job.

Noah walked across the dance floor to the desk and sat opposite her, still looking stiff and uncomfortable.

She glanced up from her writing. "Is this about us having sex last week?"

"What?"

"You're behaving so awkwardly around me. I don't bite, you know."

"Oh, well, I didn't realize I was—"

She gave him a skeptical look. "Don't bullshit me."

He expelled a sound that was half laugh, half sigh. "You're something else, you know that?"

"So I've been told."

"I suppose maybe I'm a little uncomfortable because I like to feel as if I'm in control of any given situation, and last week, what happened… That definitely wasn't me feeling in control."

"You didn't want us to have sex?"

"Oh, I definitely wanted it. I just…well, I didn't think it was the wisest choice I could have made, given the fact that we need to be able to work together amicably in the fore-seeable future."

"I thought it was plenty amicable, what happened." She kept a straight face, but she wanted to smile. Wanted to do something to ruffle that well-groomed exterior of his again.

She wanted to bring the clean-cut, dirty boy out to play.

She handed him the list of names.

"What's this?" he said.

"Those are a few employees you might consider hiring as your new assistant manager."

"Does that mean you don't want to help out tonight?"

"Of course I'll help as much as you need. Those are people I've considered for promotion. They're good, reliable employees who've been with Cabaret for years. I'd have a tough time choosing who to give it to."

"So you're leaving the difficult choice to me instead?" He smiled.

"Something like that. But I did put the person most deserving of the job at the top of the list."

"Thank you," Noah said. "This is really helpful."

He started to rise.

"Wait," she said, standing and walking around the desk to him.

"I don't want you to feel uncomfortable in my presence. What can we do to fix that?"

The jungle sounds were still playing in the background, and she realized now how ridiculous it probably sounded to Noah.

"Could you perhaps stop being so damn sexy?"

His comment caught her off guard, and she laughed. "I'm afraid not."

"Then I don't know what to do. You affect me." His gaze lingered on her mouth for a moment too long, and she understood exactly where his awkwardness was coming from.

It wasn't that he was repulsed by her. It was that at any given moment, he was feeling exactly the way she was—desperate to drag her into the nearest private or not-so-private room and screw her brains out.

She decided to test her theory. She reached out and trailed

a finger along the line of his jaw. The slightest bit of razor stubble could be felt there, and the simple contact sent a shudder of desire through her.

Noah closed his eyes and sighed. "That isn't going to lead anywhere good."

"Of course it is."

He opened his eyes as he reached up and grabbed her wrist. But instead of pulling her hand away, he pulled her to him and kissed her for all she was worth.

Ari's insides turned liquid, and she molded herself to him, desperate to feel every bit of him at the same time.

Their kiss turned into a frenzy of tearing off clothes and shoving aside undergarments. Noah hurriedly put on a condom, then he turned her around and bent her over the chair he'd been sitting on.

He mounted her like an animal. She could see them in the wall mirror, his stiff erection pushing into her, their bodies locked together, his arm holding her tight as he began pumping his hips.

Her body was wet and ready, with just that one kiss, that instant of contact, and she arched her back and felt him stretching her, touching places inside her that ached to be touched.

She braced her knees against the seat of the chair and held on to the back for support as he grasped her by the waist and shoulder, pounding her harder and harder, almost violent in his desire.

He'd have had no way of knowing why she might have hated such aggressive lovemaking, but with him, it only felt good.

It felt right.

She knew he wasn't a violent lover. She knew he was only feeling what she felt—an unstoppable need to ease the aching.

He was building fast toward release, and she, too, could

feel her body tensing, ready. Lovemaking was still new enough to her again that the slightest stimulation was all she needed.

She watched them in the mirror, savoring the sight of his strong body claiming hers. They were still half-dressed, but his shirt was open, and her yoga pants were somewhere on the floor while her tight tank top was pushed up above her bare breasts.

Noah, his hands shaking now with the nearness of his orgasm, grasped her breasts and leaned over close to kiss her neck. A moment later, he was crying out, gasping against her skin, and the intensity of it gave her the final bit of stimulation to lose herself to her own orgasm.

She bucked against him and uttered a string of curses and gasps of pleasure as wave after wave of sweet tension washed through her.

A moment later, she felt giddy with accomplishment. She'd done it.

Again.

Noah eased himself out of her, then turned her around and placed a soft kiss on her mouth before taking off the condom and tucking himself back into his pants.

He was still breathing heavily, perspiration on his brow. She reached up and wiped it away.

But he averted his gaze, and she felt another emotion besides happiness getting stuck in her throat. She got dressed and tried not to feel hurt that he wasn't interested in any post-coital bonding.

She wasn't, either, right?

Um, right. Not with Sir Sex-a-Lot, anyway.

This was exactly what she'd wanted—no-strings, uncomplicated sex. It was mostly all she'd ever wanted, all through her rip-roaring twenties.

"I really need to get back downstairs. I left a bunch of stuff—"

"It's okay. I'll be down in a bit to help out. I just need to get cleaned up and change clothes."

"No hurry," he said, heading for the door now, as if fleeing the scene of a crime. "Whenever's convenient for you."

Ari watched him disappear out the door.

So. Anyway.

Time to grow a pair and stop going around acting like she cared if her sex had strings.

Her body still hummed with the pleasure of what they'd done. That should have been enough.

But…

She knew what the problem was. Seeing Noah across the way, in his fishbowl of an apartment, he hadn't really been human to her, she realized now. She could watch him and objectify him all she wanted. He hadn't been any more real to her than a character in a soft-porn flick.

Here's the wealthy businessman. There's his latest conquest. Watch them screw. Oh, isn't that hot.

Or not.

But Noah was human. He was a guy with a brother he clearly cared about deeply, judging by the way she'd seen him interact since Simon had started working at Cabaret. She'd seen Simon in the apartment, too, but she hadn't paid much attention to him, since mostly what he did was sit on the couch or stare into the refrigerator.

Noah wasn't the uncomplicated sex object he'd been in her imagination.

And she wasn't the uncomplicated twentysomething she used to be. She was a woman who'd lost some part of herself. Her innocence maybe. Or her ability to be carefree.

She hadn't expected this. It hadn't been part of her plan to like Noah, to feel some unfamiliar urge to bond with him outside of the sack.

She slumped into her desk chair and stared across the room at the door where Noah had made his hasty exit.

What if she wasn't able to have casual sex anymore?

No, that was ridiculous. She was just feeling sensitive because she'd gone so long without a lover, and now that she had one, it was kind of a new experience.

But what if it wasn't ridiculous? What if it was true?

A WEEK ON THE JOB, and Simon could have happily never seen another dirty dish again in his life.

He shoved the full tray of dishes into the machine, then wiped his hands on his apron and headed toward the back alley for a smoke. He passed through the kitchen full of cooks and servers he barely knew, and he resisted the urge to scowl at them.

No, he was going to play the game this time—smile and act friendly and pretend he gave a damn.

He was tired of living on Noah's couch, and in spite of his annoyance with his brother's meddling in his life, he knew Noah meant well. Simon was going to do right by him this time.

Two more weeks, and he'd be moving into his new studio. Noah had even taken him to IKEA and let him pick out whatever he wanted to furnish it with. He didn't like taking handouts from his brother, but he'd make sure he paid him back later, when he had some extra cash.

Outside, he relaxed in the cool, damp air of the courtyard. Surrounded by buildings, the space set aside for employee breaks was enclosed by tall fencing covered in vines.

He pulled a pack of cigarettes out of his pocket and was about to light up when a sound from above caught his attention. He looked up at the landing outside the second floor and saw a woman step out the door. It was Arianna, the chick who'd sold the restaurant to Noah.

He'd seen her around, but he'd never really talked to her.

And something about her was oddly familiar. The way she moved, the way she stood so tall with her long hair flowing down her back, she reminded him of the woman who lived across the way from Noah. In fact, if he'd had any cash, he'd have laid a good chunk of it on the bet that she was that woman—the one he'd been painting.

And even if she wasn't, he loved getting an up-close view of her, because her face was going to be the face of the dancer in his painting.

She offered a little smile. "Hey, mind if I join you?"

Simon shrugged. "Want a smoke?"

"No thanks," she said as she descended the stairs.

Simon couldn't help but admire her. She was crazy-hot, and something about her smile said she wasn't stuck on herself. She seemed kind of like she could laugh at whatever came her way, including her own mistakes.

It wasn't hard to see why his brother looked at her the way he did, like a hungry wolf eyeing a rabbit. Simon hated the way his brother went through women, and he didn't much like the idea of Noah dragging this one back to his place, using her, then dumping her like the rest.

"Whatta you do up there?" Simon asked, nodding toward the second floor of the building.

She stopped at the bottom of the stairs and began stretching her legs. "I'm in the process of getting a dance studio up and running."

"What kind of dance? Like ballet and stuff?"

"No. Mostly belly dancing—tribal fusion, and a little bit

of cabaret. I've been teaching it for years, but I kind of let the teaching go while running the club."

"You lost me at tribal fusion," he said with a grin, then took a puff on his cigarette and blew it in the opposite direction from her.

"It's a form of belly dance that incorporates nontraditional Western style and moves."

"Is it anything like the show that was here last night—Serpentina or something like that?"

"Yes, that's it exactly. Serpentina is a perfect example of tribal fusion."

Bingo. This was his across-the-way dancer. He'd seen her practicing moves like that at home.

"Pretty hot," Simon said before realizing maybe this chick wouldn't appreciate the comment.

But she simply said, "Yeah, it is. So you're Noah's brother, right? Simon."

He nodded, trying not to be too flattered that she knew his name.

"You like working for your brother?"

"I don't have a lot of choice, seeing as how I get fired from every job sooner or later."

Simon watched to see her reaction. He expected condescension, but instead, she seemed nonplussed by his inability to hold a job.

"So you're not really the workaday type. Neither am I."

"I probably *am* the workaday type, except being a nutcase always gets in the way."

"What kind of nutcase are you?" she asked matter-of-factly, and Simon fell in love right then and there.

No one ever, ever, ever talked to him about being crazy like it was no big deal.

"Bipolar, manic depressive, whatever you want to call it, I'm it."

Arianna nodded. "How old are you now?"

"Twenty-nine, as my brother likes to remind me. Coming up on thirty any week now, which means I'm supposed to start acting responsible and all that."

"I'm thirty-two," she said.

She looked more like she was twenty-two, but Simon decided to play it cool about that little detail. He may have just fallen in love instantly, but since his brother was clearly lusting after her, there wasn't any point in both of them chasing the same woman.

That would only end in disaster, and Simon, in spite of all the ways his brother annoyed the hell out of him, was deeply grateful for the fact that Noah was the one person in the world he could always rely on.

He'd never screw with that.

But he did hope Noah could keep his dick in his pants long enough to see that this girl was worth keeping around for longer than a night.

Before either of them could think of anything else to say, the door opened and a goddess emerged. Okay, not a goddess, but a babe of monumental proportions. Hot enough to make him not feel so bad that his brother was already into Arianna.

"Hey, Sophie," Arianna said to her. "Have you met Simon yet?"

The goddess, whose pale blond hair was tied back in a sleek knot, and whose blue eyes and smooth skin weren't marred by even a touch of makeup, took in Simon and smiled. "Hi," she said with some kind of European accent. "You're the new dishwasher?"

Okay, so it really did kind of suck that at the age of

twenty-nine, he hadn't moved beyond the title of dish-washer to something a little more impressive, like maybe Emperor of the Universe, or Brad Pitt—couldn't the world use another Brad Pitt?

Simon nodded. "Just until I take the art world by storm."

Sophie smiled, which was promising, unless she was thinking what a pathetic loser he was. Or noticing that his fly was down.

No, he was still wearing his filthy white dishwashing apron, so it couldn't be a fly issue. A hell of an outfit to meet the love of his life in.

"An artist, hmm?" She didn't scoff or roll her eyes or look away in utter boredom.

No, Simon was pretty sure she was standing there wait-ing for him to elaborate. But Arianna, bless her sweet ass, did it for him. "Simon's the brother of the new owner, Noah," she offered as if this were some impressive fact. "He's being nice enough to help out since the last dish-washer quit."

"Cool," Sophie said.

An awkward silence descended on the three of them, during which Simon's mouth went dry and he developed the certainty that he smelled so much like dirty dishes that people a mile away were gagging from the stench.

"Sophie's from Germany," Arianna said, mercifully ending the silence. "Munich, right?"

"Sort of." To Simon she said, "But I moved up here six months ago from San Diego."

"Really? My brother and I came here a few years ago from L.A."

She didn't seem all that impressed by their shared Southern California history.

"Since you're both sort of new to town, maybe you should get together sometime and play tourists," Arianna suggested, and Simon wanted to kiss her right then and there.

"That would be nice," Sophie said.

She sounded as though she actually meant it.

"Yeah," Simon croaked, his throat closing up, refusing to cooperate.

Sophie was way, *way* out of his league, and he wasn't sure why Arianna was playing his fairy godmother, but he was eternally grateful to her for it.

"Well, um," Sophie finally continued, "I just stepped out here to get a bit of fresh air. Guess I'd better go check my tables."

She turned, and he called after her lamely, "Nice to meet you."

After she left, he caught Arianna staring at him with a knowing look.

"She's gorgeous, isn't she?"

"Unbelievably," he whispered, staring at the closed door now.

"You have a girlfriend?"

"Not since I accidentally set my last one's living room on fire in a little firecracker mishap."

"That's the most Beavis and Butt-head breakup reason I've ever heard."

Simon laughed. "Yeah, no kidding. Except I swear to God it wasn't my fault. She was the one who lit the firecracker. I got blamed for having brought them over along with a six-pack of beer."

She was silent for a few moments. "The thing about Sophie is, lots of guys come in here and flirt with her, fall all over themselves to impress her. But they never seem to notice anything beyond the fact that she's pretty."

"Hard not to notice that."

"If a guy wanted to get anywhere with her, they'd show some interest in who she is, and what her dreams are."

"You mean treat her like a human being?"

"Amazing how few people think to do that."

"Us twentysomething guys are kind of useless that way."

"Not all of you," she said, but he knew she was just humoring him.

"Why do you care if I get anywhere with Sophie?"

"She could use a real friend right now, you know? She's here without any family or friends, and she just went through a divorce not too long ago."

"Well, thanks for helping me out, but I'm not sure she'd even notice I existed if it weren't for you introducing us."

Ari smiled. "Sure she'd notice. I just hurried the process along. You're not giving yourself nearly enough credit."

"And you can't be her friend because…?"

"I am her friend. That's why I'm looking out for her," she said, glancing at the time on the small red cell phone she held in her hand. "Your brother's expecting me to help out. I'd better get back upstairs and change into my street clothes."

Simon watched as she climbed the iron staircase, noting the mesmerizing sway of her hips. "Thanks," he called after her. "I mean, um, nice to meet you."

He cringed at the sound of his own words. God, he was such a lame-ass. It was a wonder any woman ever talked to him. The only thing he had on his side was what the girlfriend of the fire-cracker incident had called his looks "Johnny Depp gone Goth."

Whatever that meant. When he looked in the mirror, he saw a pale, skinny guy with brown eyes and shaggy brown hair. On bad days, he saw a younger version of his mother staring back, and that scared the hell out of him.

But today was a good day. Today, in the space of a few minutes, he'd managed to fall in love, and fall in love again. Not that they were the same kind of love or anything—the first was destined to be sisterly, the second romantic.

For the first time in a long time, he felt almost giddy. And as he put out his cigarette to head back inside for the next load of dishes, he didn't have a single reason to loathe himself.

8

CLOSING TIME WAS IN SIGHT, and the evening rush at Cabaret was finally dying down after the band had played its last set. Ari's feet were killing her. As a dancer, she should have known better than to try working all night in heels, but they'd been the only dress shoes she'd had at the studio, since she hadn't gone there expecting Noah to request her help at Cabaret.

And working this shift with him had proven anything but easy. Apparently Noah had missed his calling as a dictator.

The remaining few servers and bartenders were starting to clean up their stations and do their assigned extra work. The kitchen staff was finished with their shift, since the kitchen closed at midnight and only the bar remained open for service until two.

Ari stood at one end of the bar, considering the tasks that still needed to be done. Only a couple of customers lingered at the bar, including Cara, who sat next to Ari, still looking a little sweaty from boogying down all night to the world beat. At the opposite end of the bar, she saw Simon sitting, drinking a beer as his gaze followed Sophie around. Ari had almost mistaken him for a customer without his apron on.

"Grab your drink and come with me. I want to introduce you to the brother of Cabaret's new owner. He's a hottie."

Cara looked reluctant to move. She'd just pried her feet out of a pair of four-inch strappy red heels and she likely didn't want to wrench them back in.

"I want to know who that hottie is over there. I've been trying to dance over to him all night but some other woman always got to him first," she said, nodding toward a tall man with shaggy brown hair wearing a white tunic and a pair of expensive-looking jeans who was talking to Noah. He struck Ari as the kind of guy who wore a designer suit all week and then showed up here on the weekend in faux new-age hippie gear.

"I've seen him here before with Noah. They must be friends."

They studied the two men, who finally went down the hallway together, probably to Noah's office.

Cara looked at Ari and shrugged. "Oh, well, maybe they're gay. All the really good-looking ones are."

Ari tried not to laugh. "Noah's definitely not gay."

Cara lifted an eyebrow. "You sound awfully confident about that."

"I've never once seen him bring home a guy."

"So? That doesn't mean anything."

"Trust me."

"Ari?"

"What?"

"Have you been doing Sir Sex-a-Lot?"

She considered lying, but what was the point?

"Maybe a little."

"Oh my God! That's great! You did it! You—"

"Shh! Would you *quiet down?*"

"Oh, sorry," Cara said, lowering her voice to a whisper. "I'll stop. But seriously, was it good?"

"Yes!" Ari hissed. "Better than chocolate, okay?"

"Well, since that guy I've been eyeing all night is gone, introduce me to hottie number two."

Cara picked up her shoes and her drink, and they went to the other end of the bar and sat next to Simon.

"Hey," Ari said. "Long night, huh?"

"No kidding. My brother's a tyrant to work for."

"You think? He doesn't seem so bad to me," she lied.

In truth, she was having a hard time imagining her entire staff not quitting if he didn't learn to lighten up and go with the flow.

Then again, she could be a pain in the ass herself, she supposed. And they'd put up with her for all these years.

"Simon, this is my good friend Cara. Cara, Simon."

The two shook hands over Ari, who sat between them. She leaned back to give them a little space.

"So you're the new owner's brother?" Cara asked.

"Yep, and all I got was a lousy dishwashing job."

"Doesn't say much for nepotism."

"Don't get me wrong. My brother, he's not really such a bad guy. I'm lucky he gave me a job at all, given my work history. He just wants me to prove myself by working like a dog."

Ari noted the underlying affection in his tone, and she felt something inside her soften for Noah.

"Oh, hey," Cara said as she spotted Noah's friend coming back out from the back. "Who's that?"

"Him?" Simon said, spotting the guy. "That's Tyson Carter. He and Noah are buds."

Tyson's gaze landed on them, and Simon waved him over.

"What're you doing back there? Giving my brother a blow job?"

Tyson smirked. "You want the next one?"

"No thanks, dude."

"Noah was showing me around the place."

Tyson's gaze landed on Cara, and Ari saw something spark. Simon, too, seemed to have the right intuition, because he chose that moment to do introductions.

"Sit down and have a drink," Simon ordered Tyson when he'd finished introducing everyone.

The next available seat was next to Cara, so Tyson took it, and Ari could sense her friend's elation. She turned her back to him and gave Simon a thumbs-up sign. He flashed a lazy smile and nodded, clearly aware of the good he'd done.

She leaned in close and whispered, "You've got good intuition, don't you?"

"It goes along with being crazy. My one benefit."

"You get to have artistic talent, too, right?"

"That doesn't pay the bills. It'd be better if I got some talent like understanding atomic particles or something."

"Yeah, I know what you mean."

She knew Simon's hard talk about being crazy was an insecure cover, but it only made him all the more charming. Clearly, he was the brother who'd gotten all the personality, while Noah was the brother who'd gotten all the anal-retentiveness.

"Hey, um, I was wondering something," Simon said in a low voice. "And you can just slap me if it's rude to ask—"

She laughed. "I'm sure I won't slap you. Go ahead."

"Are you and my brother hooking up?"

Ari was speechless for a moment. Was it really that obvious? She glanced over at Kip, who was restocking the fridge with bottled beer. If anyone had figured it out, it should have been him.

"Why do you ask?"

Simon shrugged. "It's kind of… Well, maybe we shouldn't talk about it here."

"It's okay with me. I don't mind people overhearing."

"It's just, you seem like a cool girl. And Noah, he's kind of a player. I just wanted to warn you is all."

"Wow, you're violating brotherly solidarity to tell me that?"

"I think he'd probably tell you himself if you asked him."

"It's okay. I'm kind of a player, too. Or at least I used to be."

The label felt ridiculous rolling off her tongue. She wasn't that girl at all anymore, she realized. She was just starting to figure out who she was now with regard to sex.

With serendipitous timing Noah emerged from the hallway and looked over to see them all sitting together. His expression somewhere between grim and exhausted, he made a beeline for their group.

"Is this night ever going to end?"

Ari smiled. "This is your first time with a band on a weekend, huh?"

The belly dance and cabaret acts were crowd pleasers, but they always ended by midnight and didn't cause customers to linger. Danceable live music, though, drew a crowd that stayed until two, and the work of keeping the place going all night was exhausting for everyone involved.

She wanted to reach out and smooth Noah's brow, or give him a back rub. Knowing how he'd probably react, she kept her hands to herself.

As if reading her mind, one of the waiters, Trent, came up behind her and started rubbing her shoulders. She didn't have to even look to know it was him. He and his legendary strong hands had given her and the rest of the female staff many an end-of-the-night shoulder rub.

Noah eyed Trent warily but said nothing.

"Should the band be breaking down already? With people still here?" Noah asked, addressing Ari.

She eyed the guy disassembling the band's sound system. "I don't see why not."

"I think it makes the customers feel hurried out the door."

She looked around. "I don't see anyone hurrying."

"And the waitstaff? They're allowed to start cleaning up with customers still here?"

"It's the only way to keep them from having to be here until after three cleaning up," Ari answered.

"I don't like it. I'm going to have to ask everyone to wait until customers are gone to finish breaking down and cleaning up."

Simon tore his gaze away from Sophie long enough to say, "Bro, lighten up."

Noah ignored him. "Can you take care of talking to the band while I talk to the waiters?" he said to Ari.

She looked at the stage. The dreadlocked guy there looked anything but hurried. The band had been professional, and they'd played a great show, and they got paid very little for their work. She wasn't about to go harass them now.

"Can I talk to you in the office?" she said to Noah.

"You can tell me whatever you need to say right here."

Trent's hands kneaded a little harder. A polite person might have disappeared at that first obvious sign of tension, but Ari would expect no less of her nosy staff than to come closer and listen in.

But this wasn't her staff anymore, not really. And if Noah wanted her to get bitchy in front of them, then fine.

"I'm not going to go harass that guy after he's been working hard all night."

"Okay, then I'll do it," he said, his face expressionless.

"Really? You're really going to be that uptight? Do you see any customers looking unhappy?"

"I've seen plenty leave already, and that's enough for me

to believe giving the impression that the business is closing when it isn't is a bad idea."

Maybe it was, but Ari wasn't feeling very agreeable. She didn't like the idea of Noah bullying her tired, overworked friends. Maybe she'd run a looser ship than he did, but at least everyone had been happy working here.

Sophie, who'd finished cleaning up her station, joined their group, sitting on the other side of Simon. Much to his pleasure, Ari was sure. And Kip, who'd finished stocking the fridge and had sensed gossip-worthy happenings, was hovering near.

"Can I get you something?" he said to Sophie.

"I'll have a vodka and orange juice," she said.

"No drinking while you're at work," Noah said and everyone looked at him as if he'd just sprouted a second head.

Sophie looked stricken. She wasn't the rebellious type—true to her German roots, she believed in following the rules and doing a good job. The idea that she was breaking a rule probably horrified her.

"But my shift—"

"Ends when the bar closes."

Sophie blinked. Simon looked like he wanted to deck his brother. "Lighten *up*."

"I'd better get going," Cara said, slipping her shoes back on.

"Where are you headed?" Tyson asked. "Did you drive?"

"Nope, I took a cab."

"Want a ride?"

Cara looked as though she might jump for joy. "Um, sure. If it's not out of your way," she said casually.

Ari knew it was all a big act. Cara was getting laid tonight, no doubt. She was happy for her friend, and she kind of envied the days when she could take a guy home and not get all hung up on him afterward.

She watched the two walk out the door, Cara's wavy blond hair springing for joy with each step.

"Sorry to be a tight-ass," Noah said, "but maybe we need to have a meeting to discuss the rules that will be enforced under my leadership."

He was sounding more like the leader of a military organization than a San Francisco nightclub.

"The rules have worked fine for years," Ari said, feeling defensive. "Is it really necessary to make such nitpicky changes?"

"It's for me to decide what's worth changing and what isn't," he said with a note of finality.

She couldn't argue. She was the one who'd wanted out of here so badly.

Sophie still looked stricken, but before Noah could say anything to make matters worse, Kip called out to the remaining customers that the bar was closing. Ari glanced up at the clock and saw that it was finally two. They legally couldn't serve another drink, and unfinished drinks had to be discarded at the bar.

The bouncer, Ernie, stood by at the front door in case anyone needed further coaxing to leave. But the remaining few customers began filing out without trouble.

Trent had stopped massaging Ari's shoulders and was sitting next to her now. She knew he wanted a beer, but no one was willing to test Noah now that he'd laid down the new law.

And it pissed her off that her friend couldn't drink a beer after working his ass off all night. She realized now that this urge to take care of her family was the real reason she stuck around after she'd sold the business. It was the people—not the place—she was reluctant to let go of. And from where she sat, Noah wasn't treating her family right.

Noah looked around at his ragtag bunch of employees, all of whom were convening at the bar for their traditional Saturday-night after-work drinks. He had no way of knowing that, though, and Ari almost felt sorry for him, having to be the heavy.

"Get to work, people," he said, looking exasperated.

Everyone glanced at each other, bewildered and annoyed. Trent made a halfhearted attempt to sing the Sha Na Na song they often sang at closing time, when everyone was just lit enough to think it was funny. He made it through one verse before everyone else's awkward silence stopped him.

Noah threw up his hands and disappeared down the hall-way, probably to hide out in his office. Ari looked at Simon and winced.

"He brought it on himself," Simon said, shrugging.

"I should go talk to him," Ari said as she stood. To the employees at the bar, she said, "I think we can safely assume our Saturday-night drinking tradition is over."

NOAH HEARD THE KNOCK at the door, but he didn't feel like answering it.

For the first time since taking over operation of Cabaret, he felt defeated. He didn't like being the asshole boss that everyone rolled their eyes at behind his back. He didn't like laying down rules and making people feel bad. And he didn't like sitting here in the office pouting like a child.

But he had little choice about laying down the law and being disliked for it when Arianna's style of management seemed to mostly involve free drinks and back rubs.

When the door opened and Arianna popped her head in, he wasn't sure whether to be apprehensive because they might end up arguing, or because they might end up screwing. Probably both.

"Can I come in?"

"Technically it's still your office," he said, hating the petulance in his voice.

She stepped inside, but before she could close the door, Simon appeared in the doorway, too. Arianna sat on the low-slung modern gray sofa that had arrived yesterday from the furniture store.

"Hey, sorry to interrupt. I'm about to take off and wanted to make sure there's nothing else you need me to do."

"No, but thanks," Noah answered, relieved his own brother wasn't still sitting out there sniggering about him with everyone else.

No doubt the employees of Cabaret operated as a tight family unit, and he was the evil new stepfather everyone hated. It left him feeling like he was on the outside of something good looking in again, with only his own sad little dysfunctional family as cold comfort.

"Okay, see you later, then."

"Simon, wait a second. You've been doing a great job. I just wanted you to know that I've noticed how hard you're working, and I appreciate it."

Simon shrugged, probably trying to appear cool in front of Arianna—or *Ari*, as everyone here, including Simon, called her. He couldn't get used to that, either, thinking of her as plain old Ari when in his mind, she was sexy, exotic Arianna.

He saw the way his brother looked at Arianna, as if she were some goddess come down to earth, and he couldn't really blame him. But he hated that she talked to Simon like an old friend. When she was with Noah, she seemed more on guard, wary.

"Well, um, thanks," Simon said. "Good night."

Noah watched as he left, feeling a lump of pride in his

throat for his brother. It wasn't easy for Simon, a talented artist and budding chef, to humble himself enough to do the dishwashing job. Noah had known this would be true, and he'd given him the job partly as a test. He wanted Simon to prove he could do whatever it took to get back on his feet.

He turned back to Ari and caught her staring at him in an odd way, almost as if she'd been reading his thoughts. "It's great that you look out for him," she said. "I like Simon a lot."

"I've been looking out for him my whole life. It's second nature by now."

"Listen," she said, "about what happened out there—"

"Clearly we have different management styles." He didn't want to hear her analysis of how he'd made such an ass of himself.

"Maybe it's not such a good idea to have me around. I think it confuses everyone about whether they're supposed to be following the old rules or the new ones."

"Maybe."

"The acts you have booked for the next few weeks will draw a much tamer and smaller crowd than tonight's. I think you'll be fine without me getting in the way."

"I didn't mean to come off sounding like such an asshole," he said, feeling compelled to explain.

She shrugged. "It's hard for me to let go of the people here. I mean, I want to keep watching over them, kind of like you do Simon. They're my family, just like he's yours."

"Fair enough. It's clear they're going to miss having you here."

"I made them swear not to throw any kind of farewell party, because it would be too depressing saying goodbye to them. And it's not really goodbye, anyway, when I'm right upstairs."

"Sure, you can stop by anytime."

"I guess so, long as everyone understands I'm not in charge. I don't think I can stand any more nights like tonight."

"Yeah," Noah said weakly, not in the mood to review the matter anymore.

He glanced at the door. He needed to get back out front to make sure everyone had actually gone back to work and weren't still sitting around talking about what a dick he was.

"Don't worry," Arianna said, as if reading his mind again. "They can close this place blindfolded. They'll get everything done."

Noah sighed. Maybe he needed to let her win tonight. He pulled a bottle of Don Julio and two shot glasses out from his file cabinet. "Want a drink?"

Arianna laughed. "That's my kind of filing system. Sure, I'd love a drink."

He poured them each an oversize shot.

Ari took hers and lifted it into the air. "To Cabaret," she said.

Noah toasted and downed his shot faster than he should have. He'd intended to sip it, but more than he wanted to savor the taste of tequila, he wanted to feel an easing of all the tension of the night. He poured himself a second shot while Ari sipped hers.

He downed that one in a few stiff swallows, and went for a third shot. Ari watched him with amusement.

"I don't fit in here," he said, as he felt himself relaxing. "It's part of the reason I think a transformation of the place will ultimately be necessary."

She crossed her arms over her chest. "I can see why you feel that way. I built this business, so it has my stamp on it, everywhere you look."

"Right, and it's obviously not the stamp I would leave."

She finished her shot, and he poured her a second. "You

hate Cabaret, don't you? You're dying to gut the place and start over."

"I agreed to your terms," he said noncommittally.

He had started out hating it, but now that he was here, he could see the charm. Sort of.

She drank down her second shot much faster than the first. Then she stood and set the bottles and glasses aside. And she climbed onto the desk, so that she was sitting in front of him, her legs off to the side, the rest of her too close for comfort again.

"Come here," she said, tugging at his arm until he stood.

She straddled his waist and cupped his hardening cock in her hand. She rubbed her palm against it, up and down, until he was fully erect. Noah expelled a ragged breath, half wanting to stop this before it went any further, and half sure there was no way in hell he could stop it.

Sex with this woman he was supposed to be keeping things strictly business with, twice in one day? Definitely addict behavior.

But maybe this counted as two days, since it was technically Sunday morning now.

Or maybe he didn't have to have sex with her at all. He could just pleasure her…. And she could pleasure him, and…

Oh, who was he kidding? Oral still counted as sex.

She undid his fly and slipped her hand inside, gripping him tight. Then she slid off the desk and he found them both there on the same side. She dropped to her knees, in yet another eerie example of reading his mind, and tugged his cock out to gain full access.

He buried his hands in her hair as he watched her mouth near his erection, and it was all he could do not to thrust himself into her mouth. He expelled a ragged breath, and she flicked her tongue out to lick him.

She slowly took him all the way into her mouth, and he nearly cried out with the pleasure of it.

Damn it, this woman knew how to push his buttons.

The buzz of the tequila overtook his brain, and he became one with the blow job, aware of nothing but the sensation of her mouth and hands working him, sending shock waves through him....

He tugged her up and spread her out again on the desk, then shoved her skirt up around her waist as he kissed her. He wanted this woman like he'd never wanted anything else in his life.

He tugged at the scrap of pink satin that served as her panties until they were out of the way, then spread her legs wide and admired her. There, where he most wanted to be, he buried his tongue and tasted the sweet musky taste of her. She gasped and squirmed beneath him, tugging at his hair as he caressed her with his tongue.

She was so slick, so wet, so close, so right where he wanted her. He slid his hand up her thigh, then found her clit with his fingertips, pulling back a bit to watch as he explored her with his hand. He wanted to see what touch she liked best, what made her squirm, what made her cry out for more.

And he might have stayed there, exploring her longer, if she hadn't sat up and slid to the edge of the desk, pulling him between her legs. He pushed her back again, but right there, with her pussy so damn close, there was not going to be any dragging this out.

He found a condom and put it on, then lifted her legs onto his shoulders as he plunged into her long and hard.

Standing like this, so that he could watch their bodies coming together, watching his cock going in and out of her, was almost too much. He nearly came before they'd even gotten started, but he stilled himself for a moment and regained his control.

Ari moved, demanding he get going again. And then he did. Slowly, slowly, easing in and out, savoring the feel of her hot folds swallowing him. Fully dressed like this except for her panties, spread out on his desk, she looked even sexier somehow, and what they were doing felt a little naughty, a little forbidden.

He slipped his fingers down past the tiny triangle of brown hair to her clit again and rubbed her until she was gasping hard and arching her back.

When he could see that she was about to come, he pumped into her harder and faster, sweat dripping down his ribs and face. Harder, harder, as if he was never quite deep enough.

Then she shuddered and bucked as her orgasm shook her. The sight of her coming brought on his own orgasm, and Noah collapsed onto her as he spilled inside her. He silenced her gasps with a long, deep kiss that tasted of tequila.

Then he lifted her, his cock still in her, and carried her over to the sofa, where he slipped out of her as he laid her down. After getting rid of the condom, he stretched out beside her and felt himself drifting off to sleep.

For tonight anyway, he felt no pain.

9

SIMON WAS WORKING HARD not to say anything stupid. When he'd volunteered to walk Sophie the ten blocks uphill to her apartment after work, he had done it for good enough reasons. He hadn't wanted to let her walk alone at this time of night, and he hadn't wanted to let her out of his sight.

He'd forgotten that walking would involve making conversation or facing awkward silence. And normally he wasn't such a spaz, but since he was pretty damn sure Sophie was the love of his life, and this was his first real chance to talk to her alone, there was a hell of a lot more pressure than usual.

He didn't do well with pressure.

In fact, he was cursing himself for not having gone back to the doctor to get his meds adjusted yet, because lately his reaction to this kind of stress was to shut down completely. Go all Coma Boy on the world around him.

This was definitely not the time to appear catatonic.

"You're so quiet," Sophie said.

"Oh, yeah, sorry. Are you cold? Do you want my jacket?"

"It's okay, I've got mine."

Right. She was wearing a jacket. Okay, next subject.

"How long have you been working at Cabaret?"

"Not long—just a few months. Ari was so kind when I came in to fill out an application. She interviewed me and hired me there on the spot. I'd already applied to, like, twenty other places."

"She seems like a really cool chick," Simon said dumbly.

He'd never responded to any woman the way he had to Ari—as if she were his sister. Maybe it was that he'd watched her, that he'd painted her, so he knew her. But he liked to think of it as something a little more spiritual than that. She was a member of his tribe.

As was Sophie. She just needed to realize it.

"She is. She was such a great boss."

Unlike Noah was the part she didn't say.

"My brother's really not as bad as he seems," he said, feeling obligated to defend Noah.

"No, he's very, um, nice," she choked out, too polite to say what she really thought.

"He was a total asshole to you tonight. You don't have to say nice things about him."

She laughed. "But you do?"

"Yeah, family and all, you know."

Simon was starting to get a little out of breath from all the hill climbing. He really needed to quit smoking, but the nicotine soothed him in a way few other things did. His doctor didn't even make that big a deal out of it since he was bipolar and therefore more screwed up than the average smoker.

"Do you think your brother will fire any of us?" Sophie asked.

"No, definitely not anytime soon. I heard Ari had it put in the contract that he couldn't fire anyone without due cause or some shit for six months. And by that time, he'll see that everyone's worth their weight and keep you."

"I hope so. This is my place right here," she said, stopping in front of a tall Victorian with crumbling purple paint.

He looked up at the house. This was the part where he should say something witty, or ask her on a date, or even kiss her.

But all he managed to say was, "Uh, nice. You have roommates?"

She nodded. "Three. It's kind of like our own little commune. They're pretty cool. Maybe you can meet them sometime."

Simon nodded. "Well, hey, you have a good night."

Sophie flashed the most dazzling smile he'd ever seen. "Good night, Simon. Thank you for walking me home."

He watched as she jogged up the stairs to the front door, her slender hips encased in tight black pants, her short faux fur jacket accenting the blond hair that hung down her back.

God, she was beautiful.

And yet, that wasn't what made him stand there staring at the door long after she'd disappeared. It was the essence of her—delicate, fragile, sweet, lighthearted—that drew him so strongly.

He turned and headed down the hill, his heart thudding in his chest, making him feel like a love-struck cartoon character.

"Sophie," he breathed. "Sophie, Sophie, Sophie."

Her name wouldn't stop tripping off his tongue, barely a whisper, and the soft, German-lilted sound of her voice echoed in his head. He loved the way his name sounded when she said it. He loved the way everything sounded when she said it.

When he finished his painting of Ari, he was going to start one of Sophie, and it would be the best thing he'd ever painted.

It would be all light and air and hopefulness.

The opposite of what he'd been painting until the dancer piece.

Ari had unlocked some part of him he'd never been willing to explore before in his work. It was the scariest part, the most vulnerable part, the part that could get hurt beyond recovery.

Just seeing her across the way, that beautiful, vibrant dancer, he never would have guessed the path he would set her on.

And now, the feeling that welled up inside him when he thought of Sophie, and how he would paint her… It was ridiculous, but it brought tears to his eyes.

He blinked them away and expelled a ragged breath. He needed a cigarette. But before he could take out the pack in his pocket, he stopped himself.

For Sophie, he would try not to smoke. No, not try. He would stop smoking. Right now.

His cigarettes would go the way of his cramped little dark paintings—they'd become relics of his past, as he became someone new.

Grown-up Simon. Thirty-year-old Simon.

Simon in love.

ARI WOKE IN THE windowless office, completely disoriented. A lamp was still on, so she was able to figure out where she was. Noah slept next to her, his arm draped over her torso. Her neck was stiff from sleeping on the hard sofa without a pillow, but having a warm body curled next to hers for the first time in so long felt really, really nice.

She'd forgotten how much she liked this part of having a lover.

She watched Noah as he slept, listened to his slow steady breathing. With his eyes closed and his facial muscles relaxed, he looked peaceful in a way he never did awake. She could imagine him as a child, probably a serious, dutiful one, but still a child nonetheless.

A surge of something painful shot through her. She wanted to know him. Not just have sex with him, but really get to know him.

But no. She already knew some key bits of information about his sex life that made the idea of getting to know him out of bed entirely too dangerous for her heart. This man was a recipe for heartbreak.

She had to remember that.

Carefully, she pushed up onto her elbow to see the clock on the wall. It was nine-thirty in the morning.

Holy crap. She was supposed to meet Lisa and Noelle, the other two members of her dance troupe, at the studio in a half hour. Both of them had a habit of being late, but Ari needed to get cleaned up and open the studio before they arrived.

She eased Noah's arm off her and sat up, then extricated herself from the couch as gently as she could, hoping not to wake him and have to face an awkward morning-after conversation.

He groaned softly and rolled onto his other side, settling more comfortably on the couch. Ari held her breath and stood still, but he didn't wake.

She went about putting on her shoes and straightening the clothes she'd slept in, then slipped out the door, both hating the idea of leaving without saying goodbye, and knowing it was for the best.

No strings attached, she had to keep telling herself. That was all Noah could be for her.

On her way up the outside stairs to the studio, her cell phone rang. It was Cara, she saw by the caller ID.

"Well?" Ari said by way of greeting. "What happened?"

"Oh my God," Cara answered in a whisper. "It was amazing!"

"Is he still there?"

"Yes, in the shower. We're going out to breakfast when he gets out."

"Wow."

"Amazing," Cara said again, and Ari couldn't help but laugh. Her friend never sounded like this about a guy.

"Just be careful," Ari said. "Remember he is a friend of Noah's. Maybe they met at the same swingers' club."

"Oh, God, no. I've already thought of that and asked him. He said they met at the gym playing basketball years ago in L.A., and now they're both living up here."

"They could still go to swingers' clubs together," Ari said, only half joking as she switched on the lights of the studio and closed the door behind her.

"He said that while Noah is his good friend, he also thinks he's a total man-whore and disapproves of the way he uses women."

Ari sighed. "Guess you managed to squeeze in getting his life story between having the best sex of your life."

"Pretty much," Cara whispered. "I've gotta go. He just turned off the shower."

Ari said goodbye and hung up, then dropped her purse on the desk and switched on some music. Not in the mood for jungle sounds, she switched through her iPod tracks until she came to an album of Bollywood music, with a heavy base beat and lots of energy.

Why did it seem like relationships were so much simpler for everyone around her? Well, maybe not everyone, but at least Cara, who could somehow meet a man, have great sex and get him to pour his heart out, all in the space of a few hours.

Meanwhile, Ari was hooking up with her own personal man-whore, and suddenly finding herself wanting more. Or did she?

Footsteps on the stairs. She looked up to see Noelle coming in the door. Time for rehearsal. They had a show next week, and were adding a new routine.

She vowed to put Noah out of her head. For now.

Once the sale of Cabaret had made it through escrow two weeks later and was official, and Ari was no longer in any way responsible for the business, it took her a while to get used to the idea. Rather than wanting to show up and oversee what was happening under Noah's leadership, she'd actually wanted to avoid the place. So other than stopping in for a few more sessions of getting Noah up to speed on operations, she'd stayed away and buried herself in getting her dance studio up and running.

So far, Noah hadn't attempted to change anything, but the day she passed by Cabaret on her way up to the studio and saw workers on ladders around the bar, taking down the chandelier, she made a beeline inside.

Noah was standing nearby overseeing the work and looking at something on his PDA at the same time.

He didn't notice her standing next to him at first.

"Why are you taking down the chandelier?" Ari said as she stared at the ceiling.

She loved that thing. She'd found it in a flea market years ago, and she'd cleaned it up herself because she'd known it would be the perfect focal point for the bar.

Noah turned to her, but his gaze remained locked on his PDA. "Just a second," he said, distracted.

He poked at the PDA with his index finger, and Ari rolled her eyes.

Kip, attempting to restock the bar at his own peril while the chandelier came down, saw her and smirked, then mouthed the word *asshole*.

He was right. Noah was being an asshole, and with her favorite chandelier being disregarded like yesterday's newspaper, she wasn't in the mood to put up with it.

"Didn't your mother teach you any manners?" she said.

"Because it's incredibly rude to ignore a person for an electronic device. The e-mail or whatever you're doing can wait."

Noah looked up. "No, my mother didn't teach me any manners," he said casually. "But you're right, I'm being rude, and I'm sorry."

"Thank you," she said, caught off guard by his about-face. "What did you ask me?"

"I asked why you're having the chandelier removed. It's perfect there."

He shrugged. "It doesn't spread light evenly across the bar. I'm going to install a series of hanging lights that will light the whole bar from end to end."

"I thought we agreed in the contract that you wouldn't change anything for six months."

"If you'll read the exact wording, it says no major changes to the *business model* will be made for six months following change of ownership, during which time you are acting as a business consultant."

"What?"

"I can get a copy of the contract for you to read if you haven't taken a close look."

"I read it," she protested, but… She hadn't, had she?

That was Cara's job. How had she let such a stupid change slip in?

But as soon as she thought it, she realized she couldn't really blame Cara. It was her business, and she should have insisted upon reading the contract. She'd been so eager to get the deal over with, though, she'd let her better judgment slip.

"Those are the terms we agreed upon verbally."

"You approved the wording of the contract. Nowhere does it say I have to actually consult you in all my decisions."

Asshole.

Asshole, asshole, asshole.

It wasn't going to do any good to say that aloud, and she couldn't think of anything else to say at the moment, so she turned on her heels and walked away, cursing with each step.

Noah was impossible, and there was no getting around that. Maybe it was stupid of her to have tried to stick around here as a consultant, especially if it didn't really mean anything.

She headed for the office, then remembered it wasn't her office anymore. Okay, then where to? The restroom? She was about to open the women's room door when she heard Noah's voice behind her.

"Arianna, wait. Could you just wait a second?"

She turned around, and he was right behind her.

"What?"

"I'm sorry. I know you're not happy about any changes I'm going to make, but I hope you can see that it's not personal."

"Of course it's personal. I put my heart and soul into this place!"

And she was talking in clichés now, but whatever. It was true.

"You decided to sell Cabaret. So does that mean you've sold your soul to me?"

"Of course not," she sputtered.

"Then do you see my dilemma?"

She wanted to storm into the bathroom like originally planned, but he was holding on to the door handle now, effectively blocking her exit.

And also, he was sort of right. What good would it do to storm away, when there was stuff coming up here that she needed to face?

She steeled herself. "You mean the dilemma of being an

asshole who's disregarding the spirit of our agreement and claiming the letter of the law is in your favor?"

"You think I'm being an asshole," he said calmly.

"You *are* being an asshole."

"Would an asshole have agreed to let you be here at all?"

"Sure, if the agreement is meaningless, if you know you're just wasting my time because you have no intention of taking anything I say into account."

"You assume that because I took down a chandelier?"

"It's not the chandelier."

"Then what else is there?"

She exhaled, trying hard not to lose her temper. There really wasn't any point in her sticking around if she couldn't at least maintain a civil working relationship with Noah.

Well, there were the employees. She wanted to be here to advocate for them. But even her ability to do that would be in jeopardy if she couldn't keep things civil.

"I'm sorry," she said, digging deep to find a scrap of sincerity. "You're right. I'm taking this too personally."

He sighed, looking at her as if she was finally talking sensibly.

Which pissed her off all over again, but she kept the anger in check. She had to, for the sake of her former employees.

"Can we agree that my decision to put new lighting over the bar was simply a practical matter and not meant to be a personal insult to you?"

"Yes," she forced herself to say.

"Good. And can we agree that it's simply difficult to watch a business you've built be taken over and managed by someone else?"

"Absolutely."

"I understand. I've had it happen to me. My first restaurant—when I sold it, I hated the changes the new owners

made. It was like they didn't get what I'd been trying to
achieve at all."

For the first time, Ari felt as though maybe, just maybe,
he had some sense inside his arrogant head. "So what did you
do?" she asked.

"Nothing. I couldn't do anything. I'd sold the place."

She took a deep breath and exhaled slowly, forcing some
of the tension from her body.

The funny thing was, she'd *wanted* to sell Cabaret. She
was relieved it wasn't hers anymore. But she also, ridiculously, wanted Noah to appreciate what she'd accomplished.

"So you just walked away?"

"Yes, I did. I understand you're very committed to the
people who work here, though, and you want to make sure
they're being valued."

"Yes," she said, her throat tight again. "I do."

"That's an honorable notion, you know."

"Don't patronize me."

"Can I show you something?"

"What?"

"Come into the office with me?"

She said nothing, but she followed him when he turned and
led her to the office.

The room was nothing like how she'd left it. She'd
cleared out her old furniture, most of which had been given
away or moved upstairs to the studio, and Noah had moved
in a bunch of sleek, modern-looking stuff. He'd had the
walls repainted—they were white now. Where her antique
desk used to be, there was now a Scandinavian-looking
table, black and minimal. Everything about his office was
minimal, and she wondered where he kept all his papers
and things.

From a white wall cabinet that she hadn't even noticed before he opened it, Noah removed a portfolio and carried it to the long, low-slung red sofa behind her.

"Have a seat," he said.

She sat beside him, and he opened the portfolio on their laps.

"I've had this dream for a long time," he said, flipping to the first page.

Ari looked at photos of postmodern architecture, juxtaposed with Art Deco buildings and old dinner clubs.

"What's your dream?"

"I want to create a place where people can dress up and go for an evening out. Where they can see shows, have dinner and, after ten o'clock, dance to live music—an all-encompassing night out like the dinner clubs of old, but with a modern take."

Ari listened and looked at the photos as he flipped through what was, essentially, a scrapbook of his dream restaurant, and she didn't want to like his ideas.

But…she did.

He had good taste. It wasn't her style, but she liked his eye for simple lines, and she liked what he wanted to create.

It was a far cry from Cabaret, though.

"What do you want to call the place?" she asked.

"Door 22."

"Hmm."

The name sounded a little snotty, a little like he was trying to be cool, but…it wasn't bad. She didn't want to admit that she kind of liked it.

"You don't like it?"

"No, I do. It's just hard for me to imagine Cabaret not existing anymore," she said, shaking her head. "I doubt I'm the person to ask what a good replacement name would be."

Her gaze landed on a note in his portfolio.

Need ideas for dessert menu.

"You're changing the dessert menu, too?" Ari blurted.

Noah followed her gaze to the note. "I'd like to. The current menu isn't as good as I'd like it to be."

"That's because the head chef doesn't care about dessert." She was sounding defensive even to her own ears. "An outside supplier was the best option I've come up with."

He nodded. "I'd eventually like to hire a pastry chef, but for now, maybe we should find a new supplier."

She thought of the pastry shop she'd been looking into as a new supplier herself, because she wasn't all that happy with the current dessert menu, either, but she wasn't sure she wanted to help Noah with the problem.

He closed the book and looked at her, his expression serious.

"You know, when I first came here," he said, "I didn't really get the appeal of this place."

Ari stiffened, biting her tongue to keep from spitting out an insult.

He continued. "But now that I've spent some more time here, I see why you've had such a thriving business. You've created a place that's warm and fun and inviting. It's hard to imagine destroying what you created."

All the tension drained from her body, and although it was possible he was just manipulating her, she was grateful to have her accomplishment acknowledged.

"Thank you for saying that," she said.

"This can't be easy for you, I know."

She nodded. Aware now that with the angry tension gone, she realized she was still attracted to Noah. This took her a little by surprise, because her interest in getting him into bed had waned in the past few weeks. The stress of her life changing so drastically had overshadowed everything else.

"But you've wanted to get away from running Cabaret, right?"

"Yeah," she said quietly.

"Why?"

Why, oh, why? The million-dollar question.

"Lots of reasons, really. But mostly because running such a hectic business takes so much of my time and energy. I'd stopped feeling like a dancer and started feeling like a manager. And that's not me."

"And now?"

Now, she had to admit, she was thrilled to be free of the responsibility. But if she admitted that to Noah, she'd be letting go of even more of her power.

"Now, I'm starting to get focused on dancing again. It feels good."

"So this is a positive change for both of us, if you can let go of the need to keep Cabaret the way it was. It really is time for you to let go," he said gently.

Part of her wanted to argue with him, to let him know she was onto his manipulative efforts, while another part of her wanted to give in, give up the fight, let it go.

Let it go.

He was right.

Her work here was done.

"I love this place," she said quietly.

"And you created something great. It's not ending—it's just evolving."

She leaned back on the couch and sighed, feeling as if a lifetime of effort had been sucked out of her.

"Why does it have to?"

"Because no one could run Cabaret except you. Without you in charge, it's soon going to start feeling like a bad imitation of the original. It may already be."

"Maybe you're right." The weight on her chest was getting lighter and lighter.

"To keep things fresh, I have to make the restaurant into my own creation."

She looked at Noah then, sitting beside her with his tie loose and his white shirt unbuttoned at the collar. His brown hair was mussed a little, giving him the look of a man who'd just had a roll in the hay. If he had, it wasn't with her.

Ever since she'd slipped out of his office two weeks ago, they hadn't slept together again. For her part, she'd kept herself in check out of confused feelings—fear that if she slept with him again, she'd get more attached.

Here was the guy she'd been attracted to from afar, her dirty little clean-cut guy fantasy. He was the exact opposite of every guy she'd ever dated, the last person anyone would guess she had the hots for.

But she did, in spite of the fact that he could be such an ass, or maybe because of it. Their differences kept him feeling safe—someone she could physically desire without her heart getting involved. Except her heart was involved.

"Do you have any free time this afternoon?" she asked.

"Yeah, I do. Right now, actually."

"Come with me," she said. "I want to show *you* something now."

10

"ARE YOU GOING TO TELL ME where we're going?" Noah asked as he followed Arianna out the entrance of Cabaret into the cool sunny afternoon.

"You ask too many questions." She slowed so that he was in step beside her, and he couldn't help noticing the way her breasts bounced a little as she walked.

Silly for that to arouse him—after all, those very breasts had been in his mouth numerous times—but it did.

She had such lush curves for a dancer, and yet the way she moved was unmistakably ballerinalike. She stood tall, with perfect posture, and her every movement, right down to the way she gestured with her hands, was graceful.

"Did you study ballet when you were younger?" he asked. "Sorry, it's another question—I know."

She smiled. "I'll forgive you that one. I did, actually. I studied everything—ballet, tap, jazz, modern, belly dance, gymnastics…. I started at age five and continued all the way through college. After that I traveled for two years studying dance in India and the Middle East."

They crossed the street at the corner and started heading south.

"You must have had pretty supportive parents." And loaded ones, too.

Noah had never taken an extracurricular class as a kid. He envied that kind of normal childhood, with lessons and Boy Scouts and sleepovers, with story time and family vacations and—

No, he had to stop that line of thinking. It was only going to get him into trouble, and it didn't accomplish anything good. He was looking forward not back. Anything he wanted these days he had the ability to reach out and take.

"My mom was a dancer, too, so she was thrilled when I showed an interest."

"And your dad?"

"He wasn't around. My parents split up when I was a kid and my mom never remarried—said men weren't worth her time."

"She gave up men altogether?"

Arianna nodded. "She was bisexual, I guess you'd say."

"So she had a girlfriend?"

"Several over the years. Then she met a French woman and moved to Paris five years ago to be with her."

"Big move."

"Yeah. I mean, she's happy, so I'm happy for her. It's all good."

Arianna stopped walking. "Here we are."

Noah looked up to see that they'd arrived at a French patisserie. "La Tarte Framboise?"

"Have you been here before?"

"No, I haven't."

"It's the city's new best-kept secret. I want you to try their signature raspberry tart."

"Because?"

"Because I thought you might find inspiration here for that dessert menu you've been agonizing over."

"I really think the problem is that we don't have a pastry chef."

"Maybe. And maybe you'll find your new chef here, or at least a supplier until you can hire the right person."

She pushed open the door and waited for Noah to step inside. They placed their order at the counter, and a few minutes later, they were seated at a tiny table next to the window, and Noah was taking a second bite of the most divine thing he'd ever tasted in his life.

He didn't look up until he'd finished the tart. When he finally did turn his attention away from his plate, Arianna was smiling at him.

"Well?"

"Wow. Do you think I can steal the pastry chef away from here?"

"I doubt it. But I happen to know that the owner's daughter, Julie, is nearly as good as the owner. She just finished culinary school and is looking for a job."

"She's hired."

Ari's smile grew wider. "She's taking a dance class with me now. How about if I set up a time for her to meet you this week?"

"Yeah, um, sure." He hesitated, torn.

"What's wrong?"

"I have to admit, I was considering saving the position for Simon. But I don't think he's ready for that much responsibility yet."

"Is he a chef?"

"He trained at a culinary academy for a year. He's quite good, but he's a little volatile sometimes."

"You mean bipolar?"

Noah blinked in surprise. "So he told you that?"

Ari nodded. "I think Simon finds it easy to talk to me."

"I'm glad you two have hit it off. Not everyone sees what's special about him."

"I have to admit, I had this idea of playing matchmaker between him and Sophie."

"That's not such a great idea." He frowned. "I think Simon needs to get settled and adjusted to the new job and apartment before he gets involved in any relationships. He needs less change now, not more."

"Are you being a wee bit controlling?"

"You're the one playing matchmaker."

"I just introduced two people who I thought might like each other."

"He's not ready. I'm only looking out for him because, if I don't, no one will."

"But he's almost thirty. He should be the one who decides if he wants to date or not."

"I'd really prefer you not encourage them. Simon gets attached, and then he sinks pretty low when things don't work out."

"But...sometimes things do work out, right?"

He leaned back in his chair. "In theory."

"You're a real die-hard romantic, huh?" Ari said, but she didn't sound all that harsh when she said it.

While Noah was grateful that she'd taken an interest in Simon's happiness, she needed a reality check.

"I've had to rush my brother to the E.R. with his wrists bleeding all over the car because his girlfriend broke up with him. She couldn't handle his being bipolar. That kind of thing can kill a person's romantic notions."

She wore a pained expression, as though she could sympathize, and he wondered what she'd been through herself that had made her so familiar with life's hard knocks. She carried some kind of burden Noah couldn't name, but he could see it in her eyes, a bit of pain lurking behind the beautiful surface.

"I'm sorry you had to go through that," she said.

"Enough of the dreary talk," Noah said as he slapped his hands on the table. "I would like to meet Julie, and I'd be happy if you could arrange it."

"Maybe if you create the position now, it'll be something Simon can look forward to moving into. Maybe he can even apprentice."

He nodded.

"So, any particular time this week I should send Julie over?"

"No, I plan on being at the club most days. Thank you for doing this," he said. "I'm not sure I deserve such help."

"I'm not sure you do, either, but I want my student to have a good job, and I think you'll take care of her."

Arianna had a definite caretaker streak, and Noah appreciated it, being the default caretaker of his own family. He watched her for a moment, and he felt himself melting.

Definitely not a good sensation. Not when he had no history of healthy relationships with women. He wasn't even sure if he was capable of having one.

Noah cast around for a distraction and eyed her slice of tart, which she'd barely touched. As distractions went, it was a worthy one. "Are you going to eat that?"

She pushed the plate toward him. "Have some. I'm kind of full from lunch."

"You really brought me here to help me find a pastry chef?"

Something in her eyes sparked. "I'll admit, I had my own selfish reasons, too."

"Which are what?"

She shrugged, gazing out the window at the passing foot traffic. Playing coy.

"Okay, don't tell me. I'm just going to sit here and eat all your pie."

"Tell me something about yourself," she said.

"Like what?"

"Anything."

"You mean, like, my zodiac sign?"

"Sure, if you want to."

"I don't want to."

"Cool, because I don't really care about that."

"So what should I tell you?"

"How about explaining why you're a financially success-ful guy who can never waste a bite of food?"

She'd paid attention to his eating habits? Again, some sentimental little part of him melted.

"How do you know I never waste a bite?"

"I've seen you scarfing down food at Cabaret in the middle of a shift. You do everything but lick the plate clean."

"Because I'm a growing boy?"

She smiled. "That's not it."

He scooped the last crumb of tart onto his fork and ate it, proving her point. "Because I remember what it feels like to be hungry," he said, deciding to be honest. "Really hungry."

"Yeah? How do you mean?"

"We didn't have much when I was a kid. We were lucky if we got dinner most nights."

Her expression didn't change. She simply watched him and listened.

He continued. "It was a good thing the schools served free breakfast and lunch, because a lot of the time that's all we got to eat."

"Your family was pretty poor, then?"

"If you want to call it a family, yeah."

"You and Simon are a family—a pretty good one far as I can tell."

"I don't know about that. Dysfunctional is probably the better way to describe us."

"Dysfunctional family is an oxymoron."

He smiled. "True enough."

"And you two seem to really love each other. You're lucky. I grew up an only child, thinking the world revolved around me," she said, her tone more self-deprecating than usual.

"What set you straight?"

Her expression darkened for a half second, so fast she probably didn't even realize it. "Just...life," she said. "You know, stuff happens, and you can't help but realize everyone's not here to make your world easier."

"Something tells me you've experienced cruelty firsthand."

She took a moment to respond. "Yeah, well...my mother drank a lot when I was growing up. She's never really stopped."

"I'm sorry to hear that," Noah said, but he was also relieved. They had true common ground. She wasn't a spoiled child with adoring parents and a squeaky-clean normal life. She'd been knocked around a bit. And she had a screwed-up mother, as he had.

"Yeah, me, too. But we don't have to talk about depressing stuff like that, do we?"

"Not unless you want to."

She gave him that look again, the one that made him think she was picturing him naked.

"I want to talk about anything but that," she said, leaning her elbows on the table.

He got the distinct feeling she was flirting with him now

in a way she hadn't before. This flirting wasn't about sex. It was about something else—getting to know each other. And while part of him was right there with her, the other part of him, the self-preserving part, wanted to run like hell.

He cleared his throat and prepared to be an asshole. "I really should be getting back now," he said, glancing at his PDA to check the time. "Lots of work to do."

He knew this would piss her off, and it did. The warmth in her gaze turned to mild disgust.

"Yeah, sure, whatever." She stood and headed for the door without even pausing to wait for him.

Instantly, he regretted pushing her buttons. Why couldn't he have been a little more gracious about putting her off?

Or maybe it had been his imagination. Maybe she hadn't been angling for insider knowledge of him at all.

No.

She had been.

If Noah knew anything by instinct, it was when a woman wanted him—and what she wanted from him. He'd perfected the art of scanning the horizon for his next conquest, dismissing any prospect who was clearly seeking commitment. Anything more than a satisfying trip to bed he simply wasn't interested in.

Until Arianna.

When he least expected it, he caught himself connecting with her—this cozy conversation about their painful childhoods was just one example. And if he wasn't careful, he'd channel Simon, getting himself trapped in the unfriendly waters of caring too freaking much. Yeah. Not going there. So much safer to keep this thing between them physical. Which—he watched her gorgeous ass swaying in her faded jeans as she scurried away—wasn't difficult.

"Hey, wait up," he said, following after her.

But she didn't turn around or even slow her pace. She simply went full speed ahead. And the way she walked—dear God. She moved with such sexual energy, it was hard to understand how she could be so hot and cold at the same time. His experience with women who moved like her was that they only had two temperatures—hot and hotter.

When he caught up to her, he said, "I'm sorry. I didn't mean to be rude, cutting our talk short."

"You didn't."

What to say? That he didn't play the let's-share-all-our-secrets game? That he preferred communication with women to be all touch and no talk? That he might be a sex addict and probably needed to seek treatment?

Um, no. He wasn't going to say that.

"It's just, well, things seem to be a little complicated between us." Yeah, complicated in that he actually did want to play the secrets game and no way could he open up all that ugly vulnerability to her. "And I have some stuff going on in my personal life that's making it unwise for me to get romantically involved right now."

She stopped and turned to him. "Who said anything about getting romantically involved?" she asked.

Had he misread that flirtatious, let-me-in vibe? Was he overreacting to simple conversation? One of the questions from those stupid online sexual addiction quizzes came back to him. Something about misconstruing casual comments as pushing for commitment then running scared from it. Check one more box for his eligibility as an addict.

"We've just had sex a few times, right?" she continued.

Right.

"I shouldn't be. Having sex, I mean," he forced himself to

say. Because wasn't that what all the Web sites suggested? Stop having sex and get help.

She looked as if she wanted to say something else but wasn't sure what it was okay to ask.

Then he realized it probably sounded like he had gonorrhea or something.

"It's not an STD—that's not why I can't. If that's what you're thinking…"

"I wasn't." She smiled. "Well, actually I was."

"Seriously, I don't."

"Okay, so that's settled." Again, she had the look of wanting to say something, but holding her tongue.

"What? Go ahead. Say what you're thinking."

"I'm confused, that's all. We've got a good thing going. We're both enjoying it. So what could keep you from being able to get involved? It sounds like a convenient excuse to me."

She began walking again, forcing him to follow if he wanted to defend himself.

"It's definitely not an excuse. Maybe I'll be able to explain someday, but not right now." How could he explain when he wasn't clear himself? All he knew was that in the time it took to wolf down a couple of tarts, he felt urges to get closer to Arianna than he'd ever gotten to a woman, and that scared the crap out of him. But he couldn't let her go. So maybe it was time to call that therapist and get his head on straight.

"Why not? I think I deserve to know."

"I'd rather not say."

"Then I'd rather not listen to this—"

"Arianna, wait." He reached out and grabbed her arm to make her stop.

She glared at his hand as though it was a splat of bird

shit. "Don't touch me," she said, jerking her arm free, then strutting away.

Noah watched her leave.

That hadn't gone well.

And he didn't know what else he could have said. He supposed he should have been comforted at least by the fact that he'd accomplished the seemingly impossible, given the way he jonesed for her. There was no way in hell she'd have sex with him anytime soon.

But it wasn't any comfort at all.

Not even a little bit.

11

ARI WANTED TO CRAWL into a dark hole and die.

Rejection, she could handle. But rejection from a guy she didn't actually like in any normal, quantifiable way?

Utter humiliation.

She took the stairs to her apartment two at a time, getting out her anger in the physical exertion.

Maybe it just went to show that she had no business messing around with someone like Noah.

Really, she didn't.

He'd done her a favor by rejecting her.

She was breathing hard by the time she made it to her floor, and once she was inside the apartment, she filled a glass with water, then drank it in great gulps.

She didn't feel much better, but she was beginning to get the smallest sense of relief that at least she'd had her lust put in check by Noah's true colors.

Nothing good could have come of her messing around with such an asshole, right?

She took off her jacket and hung it on the hook next to the door, then slipped off her shoes, too. With all this pent-up anger, now was as good a time as any to practice the new dance routine. That's what she should be doing, absolutely.

But...

Having Noah only a few feet away for the past hour, she could hardly think straight now. She wasn't only angry. She was aroused.

She crossed the room to close the blinds, and she let herself do the thing she'd been avoiding doing.

She looked across the way into Noah's window.

At first she saw nothing, but then she caught a glimpse of him in his kitchen, leaning against the counter.

It looked as if he was just standing there, not doing anything at all.

Odd.

She'd have thought he'd go back to the restaurant after their argument, but there he was, alone in his apartment... staring at the floor?

What *was* he doing, anyway?

She hesitated, then picked up her binoculars from the shelf near the window and brought them to her eyes. If they weren't going to sleep together, if they were only ever going to be enemies or at best awkward acquaintances, then what was the harm in her watching him if she felt like it?

She couldn't think of any. Besides, this was the city, and if he wanted any real privacy, he'd have closed his blinds.

She adjusted until she was looking directly at his face. And he looked utterly miserable.

Miserable?

He brought one hand to his eyes, then his temple. For a moment, he was still. Then his shoulders heaved, as if he was taking a deep, cleansing breath.

He didn't look anything like the arrogant asshole she'd talked to earlier. This version of Noah was one she'd never seen before. He looked vulnerable, if that was even possible.

It was like watching an injured lion—a sight both compelling and tragic. All that strength and beauty gone to waste.

No, stop it.

Romanticizing Noah only spelled trouble.

She lowered the binoculars but continued watching, preferring the far-away view to the close-up one, which was too intimate for a guy she didn't want to know any better.

Maybe she was taking his rejection too personally.

Whatever had kept him from getting involved with her had also stopped his revolving door of lovers lately. He hadn't been sleeping with anyone—or, at least, anyone except her.

In all the stress and upheaval of selling Cabaret, getting her dance studio together and seducing Noah every chance she got, she hadn't noticed the change in his behavior. She'd been too busy and too tired to play the voyeur, although a couple having sex in a lit window was hard not to notice.

So he'd been trying out monogamy? And if he thought he shouldn't have sex with her, did that mean he wouldn't have sex with anyone?

Had he been telling her the truth?

But what would make him shut down his personal life? She knew from experiences with her mother that Alcoholics Anonymous members swore off relationships until they'd made it through their twelve steps. Did Noah have an addiction?

Or maybe he had some horrible disease that kept him from being able to exert himself. A heart condition, perhaps?

Did doctors ever order people not to get emotionally or sexually involved?

That sounded a little ridiculous, or at least the emotional part did. She had to stop speculating, because she was only going to make herself crazy. Whatever was going on with Noah wasn't any of her business.

But… She wanted to know why he stood in his kitchen looking as if his dog had just died.

Was it her conversation with him?

She replayed it in her head, trying to recall how he'd reacted when they were face-to-face. He'd seemed okay.

Across the street he turned abruptly toward the door, as if someone had entered.

Okay, she had to look again.

She raised the binoculars and saw that Noah was talking to Simon. Noah's entire demeanor changed. His posture was more erect, his face more animated. He was masking his earlier anguish.

Very interesting.

Simon moved toward the counter, smiling, talking about something that excited him, judging by his enthusiasm. And Noah was nodding, making an occasional comment.

Such a stark change of mood…

And she could see by Noah's body language that he was happy to have his brother there. Relieved, even. She realized she was watching one of the most loving family relationships that she'd ever seen. Here Noah was, actively looking out for his brother, being friends with him, even finding him work. How many brothers did that for each other?

This other side of Noah was at complete odds with her impression of him as a heartless businessman who wasn't capable of normal human emotions. She clearly didn't understand him at all.

Which intrigued her.

But she didn't really want to be intrigued by Noah. She wanted to keep it simple.

And yet, there wasn't anything simple about him, or about their interactions. Seducing Sir Sex-a-Lot was turning out to be a lot more complicated than she'd ever imagined.

NOAH STOOD OUTSIDE the community center and told himself to go inside. After his conversation with Arianna earlier in the day, he knew he couldn't put off seeking some help for his problems any longer.

A sex-addiction support group was meeting in five minutes, and Dr. Lily Chen, the therapist he'd spoken with over the phone last week, had recommended group sessions in addition to individual appointments with her.

But maybe he wasn't really a sex addict. Was he actually going to let his bipolar brother and a couple of online questionnaires diagnose him? Wasn't there something wrong with that picture?

He sighed and forced one foot forward, then another. Then he stopped again. Maybe he should have found a group farther from where he lived and worked, in a neighborhood where no one knew him.

That would have made a hell of a lot more sense. What if someone in this group knew him? What if one of his employees, or lovers, was here?

God, this was crazy.

But he needed to do something different.

When he thought of Arianna and her undercurrent of fragility, he knew he couldn't use her the way he'd used so many other women. He had to figure out how to fix himself before he could be with a woman like her again.

And really, what was the worst that could happen if he went to the support group? Someone would find out he'd had too much sex with too many partners? It wasn't the worst rumor that could be spread about him.

Besides, half the city probably already knew it, given his penchant for having sex in the living room window.

A woman passed him, glancing briefly in his direction. She looked normal. Nice, even. Not like a sex addict. But maybe she was going to the same group.

He steeled himself and went inside the building, took a moment to look at the directory to find the correct room and headed in the same direction the woman had gone. Near the end of the hallway, he found the room he was looking for. The door was propped open, and a circle of chairs was already half-full of people.

Three men and two women sat, checking cell phones, fidgeting with purses, tapping feet. Two of the men were talking to each other, and when Noah entered the room, everyone stopped what they were doing and looked up at him.

"Hi," he said.

"You're new here?" a small, intense-looking blond man asked.

Noah nodded.

"First time coming to a group session?"

"Yeah."

The man seemed to approve. "It's intimidating at first. Who referred you?"

"Doctor Lily Chen."

"Oh, yeah, she's great. I've been seeing her for two years."

And the guy still needed to come to one of these groups? Noah decided not to state his question aloud. Instead, he took a seat next to the man and tried not to fidget.

The woman he'd followed into the building was here, too. She was staring intently at her cell phone, and Noah wondered if the people in these groups ever hooked up. It was surely against the rules, but wasn't it asking for trouble to gather a bunch of sex addicts together?

Both the women in the group were fairly attractive, and under other circumstances, he'd have been perfectly happy to take them home for the night.

But…

An image of Arianna popped into his head, unwelcome, and he silently cursed himself. He hadn't let himself get stuck on a woman in years, and it was ridiculous to pick someone like her.

She was like one of those delicate glass figurines his mother had collected, before they'd been evicted enough times that such frivolous possessions were lost or broken.

Arianna would be like that in his life. A delicate object not made to withstand the harshness of getting knocked around by everyday living.

A man entered the room wearing a name tag that read Max Feldstein, MFT. Noah knew from getting help for Simon that MFT stood for Marriage and Family Therapist. The therapist sat in a chair near the door and looked around at the group.

"Looks like we've got a small bunch tonight, and one newcomer." He turned to Noah. "Welcome."

"Thanks."

"And you were referred by Doctor Chen?"

Noah nodded.

"Since you're new to the group, and we have a few others who have recently started coming, I'll go over the ground rules again quickly. If anyone feels that they can't comply with the rules of the group, please let me know so that you can be excused."

Max cleared his throat, and one of the men, a balding guy with a serious case of bouncy foot, raised his hand.

"Yes, Steven?" the therapist said.

"Um, should we give progress reports yet?"

"Not yet. After the introductions we'll do that."

"Because I've got some good news," the man said, and Noah looked away, embarrassed on his behalf.

What kind of good news could he have for a sex-addiction group? That he hadn't gotten laid in a week? That he'd stopped boinking the secretary three times a day and had cut it down to two?

"That's exciting. Please save it for a few minutes."

"Sure, sure," the bouncy-foot guy said.

"Now, first and foremost, what is said in this group is absolutely confidential. In order for our group therapy to be effective, we must have trust between ourselves. We must feel free to say whatever we want without fear of it going beyond the walls of this room. Is that understood?"

Nods and murmurs of agreement.

"Second, we don't use the full names of other people while here, to protect their privacy. You may use first names only when referring to others, or you may make up a fictitious name if that makes you feel more comfortable talking freely. Is everyone in agreement with those rules?"

"Yes," they all said.

"Excellent. Then let's begin. For the benefit of newcomers, we should go around the room and introduce ourselves, and if you have an update to give, please do so after your introduction. Steven, would you like to begin?"

"I'm Steven," the bouncy-foot guy said, looking briefly at Noah. "I've been coming to this group on and off for two years. I realized I was a sex addict when my wife threatened to leave unless I stopped some behaviors…."

"Would you like to remind us what some of those things were?" the therapist said.

"Oh, yeah. Um, I spent a lot of time looking at porn on the Internet…to the detriment of my sex life with my wife. And it became kind of all-consuming."

That qualified as sex addiction? Noah would have thought it was pathetic…not pathological.

"And what's your update for us?"

"I started going to therapy with my wife, and we talked about how she withholds physical affection from me, which causes me to turn to porn, and then that makes her withhold even more, and it becomes a vicious cycle."

"Do you feel like your wife is the one starting the cycle with the withholding of affection?"

"At first I did, but by the end of our session, I could see that I'm not giving her what she needs physically, either."

"Thank you for sharing, Steven. Who would like to go next? Lisa?" The therapist's gaze turned to the woman next to Steven, and she glanced up nervously.

She was petite and Italian-looking, with a Roman nose, sleek black hair pulled into a ponytail and a whippetlike body. She nodded and began.

"I'm Lisa, and this is only my second week coming to the group. I recently split up with my fiancé because I had affairs with two of his friends."

Noah didn't want to find these people's stories entertaining, but he did. This was way more lurid than a daytime talk show.

He forced himself to listen without judgment as the woman talked, and after she'd finished, Max called on Noah, asking him if he'd like to take his turn.

"Sure," he said. "I'm Noah, and I guess I'm just starting to wonder if I'm a sex addict."

"What led you to that suspicion?"

"My brother accused me of being one, first. I thought he was just insulting me, but the more I thought about it, the more I started fearing he might be right."

"Did he observe some behavior of yours that led to the accusation?" Max asked.

Noah was already a little sick of Max's predictable questions. Why didn't he ask something interesting like how many lovers he had in an average month?

No, stop it.

He was here to get help, not be snide and condescending.

"Yeah, I was having sex with a lot of different women, and I wasn't really keeping up with their names or anything like that."

"Did you have any other events that pushed you to seek help?"

"A woman I met," he said without meaning to.

Noah hesitated. He didn't want to talk about Arianna here. It felt as though he would be sullying her somehow, but… If he was going to be honest, she was part of the story.

"Is she one of your partners?"

"Yes, she is. Was. Except I know I can't do to her what I've been doing to everyone else, because she deserves better. I think she wants more from me than sex."

Max waited for him to continue, and when he didn't, the therapist said, "Thank you for sharing that with us. I hope you find some help here."

He turned to the next person in the group, and Noah sat through the rest of the session feeling alternately foolish for being there and liberated by telling the truth.

Maybe he did belong here after all. Maybe talking about his problems really would help him, and maybe…

Maybe once he'd figured himself out, he wouldn't be so afraid of breaking Arianna, if he learned to handle her with care.

12

ARIANNA HADN'T BEEN to a yoga class in a few weeks, so she'd made a point of setting aside time this week to go. Now that she wasn't having to work at Cabaret nonstop, she had the energy for such luxuries.

She was on her way down the hallway of the community center for the seven-thirty advanced Kundalini class when Noah, of all people, stepped out of one of the classrooms.

She was so stunned to see him, she almost walked past without saying a word. But her brain caught up to reality, and she stopped.

"Noah?" she said.

He'd already seen her—he had a distinctly deer-in-headlights expression.

"Arianna, hi. What are you doing here?"

She held up her mat. "Yoga class," she said.

"Oh. Well, um, good to see you." He started to turn away and head for the exit.

"How about you?" she said, peering past him at the group of people leaving the room he'd been in.

They weren't dressed in exercise clothes. And the room they were coming out of was set up with chairs in a circle. A class, maybe.

"Oh, I'm just, um, attending a session," he said vaguely. Then, after a pause, he said, "A sort of class, I guess."

His awkwardness was painful to watch, and she didn't want to torture him any more. She recalled the way he'd appeared earlier in his apartment, so full of anguish, and she felt bad for him.

"Well, you look like you could use a little yoga. Want to join me?" she said, only half joking.

"No. No thanks."

He backed away, and she wished she could think of something to say to keep him around longer.

"Well, see you later, then," she said.

As she watched him hurry out of the building, she frowned at his odd behavior. Then she peeked into the room to see if there were any clues about what the group had been discussing.

On the floor under a chair, someone had dropped a brochure of the type found in hospital waiting areas and psychiatry offices, entitled *The Signs of Sex Addiction*.

She stared at the brochure for a moment, blinking dumbly.

Sex addiction?

Noah?

But as soon as she thought it, she knew it was true. She and Cara had even brought up the possibility as a joke. But the constant stream of lovers, the exhibitionist behavior, the predatory energy she sensed in him on occasion, as if he were hungry and on the hunt for his next prey.

And his refusal to get involved with her.

Noah was a sex addict. She'd always thought him a man-whore, but there was probably only a small distinction between the two behaviors. The whole idea made her feel sad for him. And for her.

She'd known better—she'd known exactly what he was like sexually—and she'd gotten involved anyway. She had no one but herself to blame for that. At least he'd had the decency to put on the brakes.

Of all the people for her to be attracted to, how screwed up was it that she'd chosen a guy with a serious sexual dysfunction?

Somehow, thinking of him having sex with all those different women, for all the world to see, had felt removed from reality. A sort of joke, really. But this brochure, this little classroom, it was no joke. It was for real.

He had a real problem, not an amusing habit.

And ridiculously, she felt a surge of protectiveness for him. She wanted to stop him from harming himself, make him all better so he could have a normal, happy life.

Ari headed for her class, but the soothing music and dim lights in the room did little to calm her. She sat on her mat stretching, not making eye contact with the others in the class, wishing she could go home and cry.

But maybe, if she let herself get lost in the rigors of this class, her mood would improve. So she stuck it out, and at the end of the hour-and-a-half session, she'd nearly forgotten her stress over Noah because she had to concentrate so hard not to collapse in pain from the challenging workout.

Exhausted but invigorated, back in her apartment, she peered out the window at Noah's place, where a light was on in the living room. But Noah wasn't there—he was probably at Cabaret overseeing the evening operations.

Simon was there, sitting next to the window at an easel, painting.

Ari watched him, feeling an unexpected pang of affection for the younger man. Simon and Noah both brought out feelings in her that were far more loving and familial than she would have liked. She wanted to be tough. She wanted to be invincible when it came to men. But those two made her feel...

They made her feel, period.

And she wasn't sure if it was a blessing or a curse.

SIMON HAD BEEN FLOATING for days, because his life, for the first time in a long time, was starting to feel normal.

Yesterday he'd picked up the keys for his studio, and tomorrow the furniture would be delivered. But more important, yesterday he'd bumped into Sophie at work and worked up the courage to ask her if she'd like to go sightseeing on her next day off.

And she'd said yes, that she'd love to find a warm, sunny beach like the ones in San Diego.

So they were in the car now, headed for Stinson Beach. It felt too good to be true, and he had to remind himself not to constantly smile like a dope.

"I've been wondering about your brother and Ari," Sophie said, keeping up a steady stream of chatter that he found soothing. "Do you think they've got something going on?"

"Why would you think that?" Simon didn't really want to answer, partly because he liked Ari and hoped she knew well enough to stay away from a guy like Noah, and partly because he was doing his best to pay attention to the road. It had been a long time since his brother had let him drive his precious Audi, and Simon was determined not to wreck it or hit anything or even get the thing dirty. He'd deliver it back in perfect condition this time.

"The way she looks at him, and the way he looks at her—something's going on. I think they're definitely hooking up."

Yeah, she was right. But he didn't want to believe it. He

felt equally split between brotherly loyalty and a desire to kill Noah if he treated Ari the way he treated other women.

"Simon?"

"Oh, yeah, sorry, I'm not so great at talking and driving at the same time."

She giggled at him. "That's okay. I can do enough talking for both of us. You just drive."

They reached the Golden Gate Bridge, which was fully visible today with no fog at all over the water. Its bright red-orange color was a stark contrast to the blue sky, and on a rare warm, sunny day like this, people were eager to get out and enjoy the water. White sailboats dotted the bay down below.

"It's so pretty," Sophie said, sighing as she pulled her legs up into a crisscross position on the seat. "I can't believe we live in a place like this."

"What's it like in Germany?"

"Dull," she said.

"And?"

"Crowded."

Simon laughed. "There has to be more to it than that."

"You're right, and I'm the one who's supposed to be talking." She laughed a soft tinkling laugh again, and his body responded as if she'd stroked his cock.

Yeah, it had been a little while since he'd had any kind of action. No joke when a girl's laughter could give him a hard-on. Though this was Sophie—he had little doubt her belly-button lint could turn him on.

They reached the Marin County side of the bridge, where the highway wound through green hills. He couldn't remember how long it took to get to the Highway One exit, so he kept to the right lane and drove slowly, annoying the drivers behind him, judging by the angry looks he was getting as people passed.

"The town I grew up in was cold and gray a lot, a little village among the vineyards of the Rhine Valley. I grew so bored of it as a teenager, though, that I left when I turned eighteen and went to Munich. The people were friendlier there than in the town where I grew up, and I had a good time in college."

"Is that where you met your ex-husband?"

It pained Simon to think of Sophie as once-married. Some stupid part of him wanted her to be all his, but he knew well enough that he was being unrealistic, especially when she wasn't "his" at all.

"Not at school, but in Munich, yes. He was at a friend's party one night, and he was the only American there. I liked how relaxed he could be hanging out in a foreign country, speaking a foreign language with his bad accent. It was charming."

"What went wrong between you two?"

"Oh, the usual. You don't really want to hear about that, do you?"

"Sure I do."

He spotted the exit and steered the car to the off-ramp. He'd only been on this side of the bridge once before, when he and Noah had done a day trip here. The whole place felt foreign compared to the concrete and bustle of the city. Here, nature still ruled. There were more trees than people, it seemed, and the rugged landscape had not succumbed to suburban housing tracts the way all the other spaces around the city had.

"I guess I discovered the truth about romantic love in my first marriage. Once it wears off, if you aren't with a person who'd be your best friend even if you weren't in love, you can really start getting tired of each other fast, you know?"

Simon wouldn't know. He'd never had a best friend besides his brother, and he definitely didn't want to marry him.

"Getting tired of hearing me talk yet?"

"Not at all," Simon said.

They reached the coast and started heading north, so that he didn't have to focus so much on looking for signs—just on the twists and turns of the road.

"I guess I know what you mean," he said. "About romantic love, I mean. I've never had a relationship last beyond that initial rush when you can't sleep and can't eat and can't imagine going a day without seeing the other person."

"Never?"

"Nope."

"If I ever fall in love again, I want it to be after becoming friends first," Sophie said.

"But how do you just be friends with someone you're attracted to?"

"I don't know. Guess that's why I haven't done it yet."

They rode in silence for a while, as Simon thought about the fact that he'd already fallen in love with Sophie, and based on her comments he could make an educated guess that she didn't feel the same about him.

Could he slow himself down enough to be friends with her now? Well, he wouldn't really have any choice, if that's the way she wanted it.

But women had a thing for his intense artist vibe. He knew that. He didn't try to cultivate it. No one who was actually crazy went around trying to seem more that way. People like him tried to hide their not-so-stable side if they could, and if they couldn't, it only meant they were too far gone to do so.

They reached the turnoff for Stinson Beach, and as they made their way to the parking lot, Simon was relieved to see that it was sunny here, too.

"We're friends, right?" Sophie said, out of the blue.

"Yeah, right," Simon answered, his throat a little tight.

He was being ridiculous. He shouldn't be letting her categorizing them as friends get him down. He needed to focus on what was going right about this day—he was with a beautiful woman, a person whose company he loved, and they were going to the beach on a rare, warm sunny day. What was there to brood about?

Nothing. He had to keep reminding himself of that and not let anything drag his mood down.

Nothing, nothing, nothing to brood about.

"Something's upsetting you," Sophie said as they approached the sand.

"Oh, it's nothing. I'm just…" He spotted a sign warning of shark attacks. "A little freaked out by sharks."

Which was true.

"But we're not going in the water, and they won't crawl up on the beach to bite you, silly."

Simon smiled. "I guess. It's the thought of them, you know. A friend of mine in Southern California was bitten by one, and I haven't been interested in surfing since."

They reached the end of the sidewalk, where the sand dunes began, and they paused to take off their shoes and roll up their pant legs.

"I want to surf," Sophie said, as if realizing it for the first time.

"Yeah?"

He noticed her feet, which were smooth and pale, with shiny blue toenails. They were so beautiful—the kind of feet a guy could turn into a fetish.

"Yeah. It seems like such freedom, to be out there riding waves."

"Just seems cold to me."

She laughed, and he noticed for the first time that she had

a bit of a gap between her two front teeth, and a little overbite. The imperfection only made her more captivating.

"You know," she said, "you remind me of my sister in Germany. She used to have a dark, brooding side."

"Used to?"

She went silent for a few moments. "Yes," she said. "She committed suicide."

"I'm sorry."

"It was very sad. She…she never managed to be a happy person for long. She had what I think you call manic depression."

Simon stiffened. Ahead of them the beach spread out in both directions, glimmering white in the midday sun, and gentle waves broke not far from shore, with the wide blue ocean going on forever into the horizon.

But he hardly registered the breathtaking beauty.

"She was bipolar?" he said.

"Yes, that is what you call it now. I forgot."

Her sister was bipolar. What kind of cruel world was it that delivered to him a woman he could love who'd already endured losing her sister to the dark size of crazy?

"Wow," he said, his throat going tight.

He had to tell her now, because later would be too late.

They walked until they'd reached the wet part of the sand, where they could walk with the water lapping at their feet.

Simon was growing tenser by the second, knowing he had to tell her the ugly truth. There wasn't any other way to do it.

He cleared his throat and tried to make his mouth work.

"Sophie, um, I have to tell you, I'm afraid I have that in common with your sister."

"What?" she said, frowning.

"Being bipolar."

Her eyes widened. "*You're* bipolar?"

"Yeah. I mean, I'm on meds, and they keep me pretty stable, but I thought you should know."

"Sure," she said. "I guess…I guess it makes sense why you'd remind me of my sister a little then, huh?"

He smiled, but he was sure it looked more like a grimace.

"Maybe it's a sign," she said, her eyes painfully wide and innocent-looking in that moment. "Maybe we're supposed to be in each other's lives. You know, like, I lost my sister, but…"

"You gain me? That doesn't sound like such a good deal."

Simon liked this line of thinking better than what he'd initially pictured—her storming away hurt and disgusted.

She smiled, then reached out and took his hand, holding it as they walked. He knew better than to think it was a romantic gesture on her part, but…it was a start.

"You believe in signs?" he said.

"I didn't used to. But some coincidences that have happened to me are too bizarre, too unlikely, to be only coincidence."

Simon thought of the unlikelihood of his falling for a girl whose sister was bipolar, too, and he nodded.

"I knew there was a reason I was drawn to you. I think you fill a little of the hole that was left when Anja died," she said.

Okay. This was good. He could work with this.

Whatever hole she needed filled, he was there.

"I'm glad," he said.

She smiled, dazzling him all over again with her pale, delicate beauty. She was like one of the points of light on the waves, glimmering and ethereal, hard to grasp and hold.

Maybe he shouldn't have even been trying.

But he was an artist. He couldn't help being drawn to the beautiful. He craved it.

Craved her.

"Tell me about Anja," he said, and as she began to talk, he felt some restless part of himself settle.

He felt okay. Again.

13

"HELLO, NOAH. Please have a seat."

Noah stepped into Dr. Lily Chen's office and looked around at the warm putty-colored walls and the overstuffed furniture in neutral tones. He chose the sofa facing her large armchair, noting the box of tissues on the table nearby. Was that for his eventual tearful breakdown?

He'd always imagined therapists like this one feeling as if their job was complete when the patient finally descended into sobbing confessions of childhood angst.

It wasn't going to happen.

"So," Dr. Chen said, "I understand you're not happy with the support group I recommended?"

Noah shrugged. "Mostly because I bumped into a woman I know from work while I was there. She takes a yoga class in the same building."

"Was that awkward for you?"

"Yeah, especially since we've been sleeping together." He surprised himself with the admission, with the honesty. Until the words came out of his mouth, he'd expected to be careful and reserved—partly because he wasn't completely convinced of the self-diagnosis and partly because life with his mother and Simon had made him fiercely protective of his privacy.

"When was your most recent encounter?"

"A few weeks ago, I think."

"You think?"

"I haven't been keeping a detailed sex log. I slept with her three or four times, I guess. And then I stopped."

Dr. Chen nodded and made a note on the pad of paper on her lap. "What made you stop?"

"Guilt, I guess. I started feeling like, you know, like I was behaving like a sex addict."

The doctor nodded sympathetically.

"And is she someone you're interested in romantically, as well?"

"What do you mean?"

"Do you have feelings for her that aren't sexual in nature?"

"I guess I do," he said.

"But the two of you haven't explored a romantic relationship yet?"

"No, not yet."

Dr. Chen watched him for a moment, seeming to choose her next question with care. She was an attractive woman, in her forties maybe, with a serious, unanimated face. She'd make a great poker player. She wore her black hair in some kind of twist at the back of her head, and her grey suit and white shirt were meticulously crisp.

She was the kind of woman, under other circumstances, he might have fantasized about mussing up and seeing if she was as formal and stiff in bed as she was on the surface. But these days, surprisingly, his fantasies didn't stray beyond Arianna.

"Did you gain any insights from your visit to the sex-addiction group?" she finally asked.

"I suppose. I mean, I figured out that I didn't want to be there."

"The reason I recommended it is addictive behaviors are

often hard to control without some external structure. That group can provide the structure you may need."

"I don't really think I'm a true addict, frankly." Even as he said it, he didn't believe himself, but he wanted to challenge the doctor. "I mean, I decided to stop having sex, and I stopped."

"What would you call yourself, then?"

"I don't see any point in putting labels on myself."

"I understand. In this case, the label is useful if it helps diagnose and treat a problem. Are you saying you don't think you have a problem?"

"I do have a problem or I wouldn't be here. I'm just saying, I think I can quit without going to any support groups or twelve-step programs. It's not my style to depend on other people for help. I grew up taking care of myself, and I can take care of myself now, too."

She let the silence hang in the air between them like a bad odor.

"What would you like your goal to be for our time here together?" she finally asked, her voice pleasant and neutral.

"I want to stop having sex with so many women. And I guess I want to understand why I was doing it so I don't repeat the pattern somewhere else in my life."

"That's a good goal statement. How will we know when we've succeeded in the first part? When you've stopped having sex indiscriminately for a month? Six months? A year?"

"I wouldn't call my behavior indiscriminate. I was choosy about who I took as a lover." His defensiveness sounded ridiculous even to his own ears.

"Excuse me. Let's disregard that word, shall we?"

"Okay, so…I've already gone probably two weeks without having sex. How about if I tack on another month? That seems like enough time to prove I'm not compulsive about it, right?"

She thought for a moment. "It depends. I think it would be best if you can remain celibate for a while longer. We don't have to choose an arbitrary period of time. Maybe we should just see how our sessions together go, if you choose to keep seeing me."

Noah wasn't all that thrilled with the idea of an open-ended sexual moratorium, but he nodded. "Okay."

She made another note on her pad. "And how will we quantify your restraint? Do you feel like any romantic involvement—including nonsexual interactions—lend themselves to your compulsive behavior?"

"I don't know. I don't really have romantic relationships."

"You only have sex?"

"Yep."

"And you'd like to reach a point where you can have monogamous relationships that aren't based entirely on sex?"

Did he? Well, that was why he was here, wasn't it?

"Yes," he said, thinking of Arianna and that sensation of melting he'd experienced at the patisserie. Those moments before he'd freaked out had been cool and he wanted to experience them again. With her.

"You said you're possibly romantically interested in your most recent lover?"

Noah nodded, his throat tightening unexpectedly.

"In what ways do you interact with her now?"

"I see her at work sometimes. I've been able to resist her, if that's what you're asking."

He sounded way more confident than he felt, however.

"So shall we say that for the time being you'll abstain from sex? After we've mutually agreed upon a date, you'll work on only having one lover at a time—and only in committed relationships."

"Um, okay." It wasn't as if agreeing with her now bound him to his word, anyway. He'd do what he damn well pleased, but at least for the moment, he felt like he had a path out of the mess he'd made of his personal life.

Dr. Chen nodded. "That sounds quite reasonable to me."

Okay, great. So he had a plan. Now he just had to stick with it.

Which was going to be no problem as long as Arianna stayed far away.

NOAH OPENED HIS EYES in the darkness. He was sweating and tangled in his sheets. His heart was racing as if he'd run a marathon, but he'd been sleeping. Actually, having a nightmare, which explained the sweat on such a cold night.

He looked around at the outlines of familiar shapes in the room and his brain slowly made sense of reality. He was home, in San Francisco—not in L.A. looking for a shelter with enough space for a family of three.

He'd been having the same bad dream for years, in which he was a kid and his family had been kicked out of their apartment. They had nowhere to live, no food to eat, and he and Simon were desperately hungry, scrounging for discarded scraps behind restaurants and grocery stores. At their worst, they stole whatever would fit inside their jackets—a package of doughnuts or a box of cereal, usually.

He'd never been caught stealing, but he'd always felt guilty about it. And while his mother never condoned such behavior, she also never asked where the food came from.

Noah, mouth dry, untangled himself and got out of bed for a drink of water. Outside his bedroom door, the TV was on, and Simon was there, surfing the Internet on the laptop while he half watched some late-night infomercial with the sound turned down. It seemed to be advertising a juicer, or maybe a food processor—something that required lots of vegetables.

For a moment, Noah was confused by his brother's presence. Why wasn't he at his studio now? Then he'd remembered Simon showing up earlier in the evening to have dinner together. He hadn't bothered leaving.

Any other night, Noah might have been annoyed, but because of the nightmare, he was grateful that his brother didn't like being alone and would probably forever show up at all hours uninvited.

"Hey, bro," Simon said. "It's a little early for you, isn't it?"

"Bad dream," Noah mumbled.

"I'm just about to hit the sack myself," Simon said, yawning. He rarely went to bed before four or five in the morning lately, and Noah couldn't help wondering what had brought on the extreme night-owl habit.

"What're you staying up so late for, anyway?"

Simon shrugged, his gaze still glued to the computer. "Crazy in love, I guess. I don't need much sleep these days."

Noah blinked at this news. "In love with whom?"

"You won't approve, so it's better if you don't ask."

Noah downed a glass of water in one long drink as he contemplated this information.

"Since when am I the girlfriend police?"

"Since you started going behind my back trying to keep me from having one."

His face, already flushed, burned at the accusation, because it was true. He'd been busted. But how had Simon heard?

"Why do you say that?"

"Because Ari told me she wasn't allowed to play matchmaker for me anymore. She said you warned her that I'm too crazy for normal chicks."

"That's not what I said."

"It might as well have been. I caught your meaning."

Simon's tone suggested he was hurt by Noah's betrayal. And of course he would see it as a betrayal, not as his brother looking out for his best interests.

Simon didn't remember, or at least wasn't so haunted by, the ugly memories of their past. Somehow his bipolar disorder gave him a whole different set of demons to battle. Leaving Noah the dreams of starvation and homelessness.

Noah exhaled an exasperated breath, put down his empty glass next to the sink and flipped on the kitchen light. Blinking in its sudden brightness, he tried to clear his sleep-fogged brain enough to respond sensibly and perhaps convince Simon that he really did have his best interests at heart.

But he was still consumed with the lost, desperate feelings of his nightmare, so clearheaded thought was unattainable.

"Want some breakfast?" he offered, hoping to smooth things over with an omelet.

Simon cast a hostile glare at him. "I'm not hungry. I'm about to go to bed, remember?"

"How about some herbal tea, then?"

Aware that he was starting to sound like a busybody mother, Noah drew the line at offering warm milk.

"Are you for real?" Simon grabbed the remote and shut off the TV. As he rose and headed for the bathroom, Noah went to the fridge and pulled out two bottles of pale ale. His brother would never turn down a cold beer.

When Simon came back out, Noah said, "I've already opened a beer for you."

"I'm not supposed to drink, remember? Might screw with my meds."

"One beer won't kill you."

His little brother made a beeline for the table in spite of his arguing, and a bit of Noah's tension turned to relief.

Simon jerked out a chair and assumed a slumped position, then took a drink of his beer.

"So you're in love with Sophie?" Noah ventured.

"Pretty much, yeah." Simon seemed to try to sound nonchalant about it, but even in his effort, his face lit up a little at the mention of her name.

"And she knows how you feel?"

"I'm not so sure about that part."

"Do you think the feelings are mutual?"

"If I knew that, I might not be sitting up all night waiting for her to call me or e-mail me or text me."

Noah tried to remember what it was like to care that much about hearing from a woman. He hadn't felt that way since… He couldn't remember when.

"How long have you two been dating?"

"We're not officially dating. We went to the beach the other day when you loaned me your car, and we see each other at work, and…" He shrugged. "She's way out of my league."

Noah pictured Sophie, with her pale blond hair, blue eyes and delicate frame. She was quite pretty, but Simon had never expressed any concern about his ability to measure up before.

"Where'd you get that idea?"

"She's…you know…not crazy."

He took another long drink, and Noah wished he'd kept his mouth shut to Arianna.

"I was only concerned about you having any emotional upheaval with starting a new job and getting your new place. I thought too many changes at once might be a bad idea. It had nothing to do with you being good enough for Sophie. Of course you're good enough."

"You were automatically assuming she'd break my heart."

"No, I wasn't," Noah sputtered.

But he was. He couldn't let go of feeling like doom was always just around the corner for Simon, the way it had been for their mother.

"I'm not Mom," Simon said. "I'm not like her. Just because we're both bipolar—"

"I know. I'm sorry. You're right. It's just, after what happened last time you had a bad breakup—"

"I'm not going to do that again."

"Good. I really am sorry for what I said to Arianna, you know."

Simon seemed not to know what to say to Noah's quick surrender. He looked as if he wanted to keep arguing.

But Noah headed off further recriminations. "I had the nightmare again. That's what woke me up."

"Same one as always?"

"Yeah."

"Damn. You think you ought to start seeing Dr. Lehman about that?"

Dr. Lehman was the therapist who saw Simon every week to monitor his moods and his medication. Noah didn't mention that he'd already started seeing a therapist of his own.

"No. I know what the dream means."

"But you don't know how to get rid of it."

Noah shrugged and stared at his beer bottle. "Do you ever miss Mom?"

"Sure. Especially, you know, at Christmas and stuff."

"Sometimes…I don't miss her. Sometimes I'm glad she's gone so I don't have to worry about her anymore, and I hate admitting that."

He expected Simon to call him out for saying something

so crappy, but his brother merely nodded. "Fair enough, man. I've felt that way, too, sometimes. You were the one cleaning up her messes, being the parent when you were just a kid. That's a lot to take on."

"Remember that Halloween when we got to go trick-or-treating dressed in old sheets, and we got all that candy, and then that was all we had to eat for days afterward?"

Simon laughed bitterly. "Oh, yeah. I remember being so happy the first day, and by the third day I never wanted to see another chocolate bar in my life."

"I still can't eat candy corn."

"I forget—why wasn't there any food?"

"Mom disappeared for a couple of days, then came back sick with a hangover."

"Oh."

"There wasn't any food in the house and no money to get more."

Simon shook his head. "Poor Mom. She never should have had kids."

"No, more like our dad shouldn't have bailed out on her—on us."

"Yeah, but he didn't realize what he was getting into when he hooked up with her."

Their mother's bipolar disorder wasn't diagnosed until her mid-twenties, after she'd already married their father, had Noah and was recovering from giving birth to Simon.

"I'm pretty sure the wedding vows go, 'for better or worse,' not 'for better or until things get messy.'" Which was pretty much why Noah avoided relationships. Things always got messy.

Simon had never been willing to completely hold their father, Will, accountable for his actions, and Noah knew it was because he didn't have any memories of the man. If Simon had, he'd have understood that the guy wasn't worth idealizing.

"Don't get me wrong—I sympathize with Mom, especially now that I'm sort of in her shoes, worrying about someone not loving me because I'm defective."

"We're all defective, and we all have that same fear."

Simon stared at him, his expression softening. "Hey, you know, Sophie was wondering if there's something going on between you and Arianna."

"Us? No, no way," Noah said a little too quickly.

"Dude, if you treat her like you treat all those other chicks—"

"Don't say it," Noah said. "You don't need to say it. I'm not, and I won't."

"There's something about her," Simon said. "She's not all brazen like she pretends to be."

Noah nodded. "I know what you mean."

"Some guys in the kitchen say she doesn't ever date anyone, like, ever."

Noah pretended not to be interested in this information, but inside, his every cell went on alert. This was a piece of the Arianna puzzle that he'd not seen before. Never dated anyone?

"Maybe that's just at work. Some people like to keep those things separate, especially since she's the boss."

"No way, man, they said even her friends don't understand why she never dates."

Noah thought about Arianna telling him her mother was a lesbian. Could it be that she was gay, too?

Not a chance.

Then why no one else? And why him, now?

He and Simon stayed up for a while longer talking about less intense, everyday stuff. The conversation was exactly what Noah needed to unwind—obviously Simon wasn't the only one who didn't want to be alone.

As Noah settled in bed, his thoughts circled to that tidbit about Arianna and dating. How was that even possible? And why him? Why now? It was a puzzle he couldn't even begin to solve.

14

ARI WAS LIVING HER DREAM.

Her new dream, that is.

It felt so liberating not having the daily grind of running Cabaret that Ari woke up each morning excited. She felt more like dancing than she had in a long time, too, and she practiced every day—in her apartment, at the studio, in the shower, even.

Scheduling classes, collecting tuition, advertising, paying bills and all the other tasks involved in running a dance studio—even a small one that was just getting started—required Ari to put in her fair share of pencil-pushing time. But the efforts were nothing compared with the admin work she'd been forced to wade through every day for Cabaret. Even finishing the class schedule was a breeze compared to the nightmare of juggling a larger staff's requirements for certain nights off. And how thrilling it was to see her time laid out before her occupied mostly by dancing and teaching dance.

She heard a tap on the studio's door and looked up from her desk to see Sophie staring through the window at her. Ari motioned for her to come in, then remembered too late that she'd locked the door. Crossing the room, she wondered what Sophie was doing up here at this hour of day.

"Hey," she said as she opened the door. "Did you finally decide to take a class with me?"

Sophie smiled. "Not now, but maybe as soon as I can save a little extra money. Do you have a minute to talk?"

Ari stood aside to let her in. "Sure. I'm glad you came up. Want some coffee? I've got some fresh-brewed in the back room."

"Oh, um, no thanks." Sophie glanced around, looking awkward.

"Have a seat," Ari said, gesturing toward the chairs beside her desk.

She perched herself on the desk as Sophie sat. "Is everything okay?"

"Not exactly. I mean, I'm just…"

"What's wrong?"

"Boy troubles," Sophie said with a sigh.

"Is this about Simon?"

Sophie's pale cheeks turned pink. "Yes, sort of."

"How are things going between you two?"

"He's acting like he's falling in love with me," Sophie said as if it were the worst possible thing that could happen.

"And…you don't want him to?"

"No." She paused, seeming to consider the question further. "At first I did, but now I don't think I do."

"So you're not interested in him?"

"No, I am! I mean, I think he's great, and we have such a good time together, but—"

"He's bipolar?"

"Maybe that's part of it."

"He's perfectly fine as long as he takes his medication, you know."

"I know. I do. I mean, my sister had the same illness so…"

"You sound like there's something more going on."

"As soon as I felt myself falling for him, I realized I couldn't do it. He's the first person I've let myself care about since my divorce, and it's too scary. I feel like there's no such thing as happy endings anymore."

Ari blinked at this idea. "I don't know about happy endings. I mean, you're young and you've got your whole life ahead of you. Maybe it's good to be content with a happy beginning for now, and see what happens."

Sophie shook her head. "I can't go through another divorce. And the only way to avoid it is to never get married again."

"Well, it's not as if Simon's proposing to you—" Then Ari got a twinge of doubt. "He didn't propose to you, did he?"

"Of course not."

"How long has it been since your divorce?"

"Two years."

Ari thought of her own recent two-year anniversary. What was it with that number?

"And you haven't fallen in love with anyone in that time?"

"I haven't even dated anyone."

"Oh, wow. I didn't realize… We have more in common than I knew."

Sophie frowned. "You're divorced, too?"

"No, but I've…"

"Some people at Cabaret say you're a lesbian, but I said no way. If you were, you'd have a girlfriend."

Ari laughed. "Believe me, I've thought about it. But I just can't get excited about anyone who doesn't have a penis."

"Tell me about it. I wish I could, but I can't. Women are so much nicer in every other way."

Ari nodded, relaxing a bit. "Something traumatic happened to me a few years ago. I haven't let anyone get close to me since. So I can relate to your fear of the whole thing. Getting hurt, I mean."

"It's awful, isn't it? Being unable to let yourself go like when we were young."

"I hate to break it to you, but we're still young. Especially you."

"I'm twenty-*eight!*"

"Maybe in Germany that's considered over the hill, but here in the U.S., it's regarded as barely past your teen years."

"Men want twenty-year-olds."

"That's not true of most men. And whomever it is true of, they're not worthy of you anyway."

Sophie shrugged.

"You can't really expect to never fall in love again, can you? Just to avoid getting hurt?"

"Why not?"

"Because then you're not really living."

As soon as the words left her mouth, Ari realized they applied to her. Was she really living, when she limited herself to getting involved with guys like Noah who broke out in hives at the hint of emotional intimacy? She could pretend all she wanted that the problem was his, but she chose him. She was the one playing it safe.

How could she be such a hypocrite, giving Sophie advice she herself couldn't follow?

Sophie stared at the shiny wood floor as if mesmerized by it. "Maybe you're right," she finally said, sounding unconvinced.

"I do know how you feel. It's much easier for me to tell you what to do than to go out and live by my own advice."

Sophie gave her a coy look. "Is there something going on between you and Noah?"

"Not really."

"But you're having sex."

"No…not anymore."

"But there's so much chemistry between you two. It's crazy, like crackling when you two are both at the restaurant. Everyone notices it."

Ari was mortified. "Everyone?"

"Of course. Especially since you've never been interested in anyone."

"Do people think…"

"No one knows what's going on. There's just some specu- lation about the two of you being locked in the office together. I was kind of hoping you'd give me some better gossip than you have."

Maybe it was time for her to change. Time to stop being afraid and start living. If Noah was the only guy she could get excited by, then she had to summon the courage to pursue something deeper with him.

And if Noah wasn't willing to have more than sex with her, maybe it was time to find a guy who was.

ARI DIDN'T KNOW WHAT she was going to say to Noah or how she was going to say it. But she was determined to find him and talk to him.

She stepped inside Cabaret, but the only person in the front of the house was Kip.

"Hey, you," he said. "Long time no see."

"Hi, Kip." Ari crossed the room to the bar. "Is Noah around?"

"He just stepped out, said he'd be back in a few. In the meantime why don't you hang out and fill me in on the latest?"

She pulled out a stool to sit. "You should come up and take a class."

"Ooh, I'd love to. We could start the first all-male belly dance troupe. What do you think?"

"Fabulous."

"Want a drink?" he asked.

"Sure, I'll have a dirty martini."

He smiled. "Going for the hard stuff so early in the day? Interesting."

"Trust me, I need it."

"This must be good."

She sighed. "Maybe. If I have any good gossip, you know you'll be the first to hear it."

"I'd better be. Hey, I've got some good gossip."

"Oh, yeah?"

"I overheard the boss man talking on his cell phone the other day," Kip said, leaning in close and lowering his voice. "He was making an appointment with a doctor I happen to know treats sexual dysfunctions."

"Oh?" Ari said, trying to look surprised. "And how do you know that?"

He made a little face, annoyed at himself for getting busted. "Because a *friend* of mine saw her for a while for a little issue he was having. Nothing serious. The point is, it sounds like either Sir Sex-a-Lot is trying to turn himself into Sir Sex-a-Little, or else he's got some even bigger kink going on than sleeping with a different woman every night."

A movement from the kitchen doorway caught Ari's eye, and she looked over to see Noah standing there staring at them. He looked, if not angry, at the very least mildly annoyed.

"So, do you think he's into underaged minors? Or maybe he—"

"Kip," Ari said, nodding in Noah's direction.

He looked over, spotted him and visibly shrank.

"Oh, Noah, hi," he said. "We were just gossiping about a friend of mine."

Noah's expression got even grimmer. "I heard what you said."

"It's my fault," Ari said. "I started the gossiping, and my doing it encouraged the behavior. Please don't blame Kip for this."

"Sir *Sex-a-Lot?*" he said, crossing his arms over his chest.

"Noah, we're both very sorry."

"For the record, I'm not into minors, or farm animals, or anything very interesting. That's all I'm going to say about the matter."

Kip said nothing.

"I'm going to leave now. I'd appreciate it if your conversation about me doesn't continue after I walk away." Noah left after shooting them a disgusted look.

Ari wanted to kick herself. If she'd been hoping to spark something between them, she'd managed to accomplish the exact opposite.

She stood and followed him toward the office.

"I need to talk to you," Ari said to Noah's back.

He stopped for a moment, then turned to look at her.

"To me, or about me?" he said.

She pushed past him to enter his office.

"To you, of course," she said quietly, letting her half-lidded gaze linger on him.

He looked away first. But he did close the door, giving them some privacy.

"I want you to let me out of the consulting clause in the contract," she said. It was a bit of a lame excuse, but being released from the contractual obligations would put them on equal footing.

Noah sat up a little straighter on the edge of his desk. "You do?"

"Yes. I thought about what you said, about how the place needs to evolve to stay fresh, and you're right. It does. You don't need me looking over your shoulder clinging to something that used to be."

"I'm glad you feel that way, but, you know—" his expression turned a little ironic "—the longer I hang out here, the more I like it the way it is."

"You do?"

He nodded. "I don't know if I'll renovate the place or not. But frankly, business is humming along so well, I'm inclined to keep it as is."

This was the last thing Ari had expected to hear. She didn't know what to say.

"I would like it if your dance troupe could appear more often. I'm hoping now that you have a bit more free time, you'd be willing…"

"Of course," Ari said, flattered.

This was going better than she'd hoped. And being in here alone with Noah again reminded her of the last time when they'd slept on the couch. She missed that intimacy.

"One other thing," Noah said.

"Yes?"

"I was hoping we could have dinner together soon. Maybe tonight?"

"Sure." Why was everything she wanted suddenly falling into her lap now so easily? There had to be a catch.

They agreed on a time for her to show up at his place. As he gave her directions she had to draw on all her discipline to not let on she was well acquainted with the location of his apartment. Maybe herein was the catch. No matter how she felt about Noah, to be with him meant always worrying that she was only the next woman in his window, and that soon enough she'd be replaced by someone else.

But now that she understood he was broken, just like her, she wondered if they might be able to fix each other.

15

NOAH HAD A SPECIAL DINNER prepared by the chef at Cabaret. He lit candles, put on soft music—the whole routine.

It was a routine he rarely performed. Sure, he occasionally had dinner with a woman before taking her home and screwing her brains out. But Arianna, he knew, couldn't be only about sex anymore. He had to make this something more.

And okay, he wasn't exactly following the rules Dr. Chen had laid out for him, but what the hell. Talking to Arianna in his office had felt good and right—even with the gossip incident—and he'd acted on impulse, inviting her for dinner.

When she arrived, looking more vulnerable and beautiful than he'd ever seen her, wearing a skimpy black tank top and skirt that hugged her curves, her hair hanging down over her shoulders and breasts, he knew he wasn't going to be able to control what happened tonight, that he was entering unknown territory.

"Wow," she said, looking around his apartment. "This is beautiful."

"It's mostly about the view," he said, leading her across the room to the wall of windows.

"Oh my God, you can see everything from here."

"How about your place?" he said, and if he wasn't mistaken, she stiffened a little. "Do you have a good view?"

Probably she was thinking he was being a little rude, and he supposed he was. Sometimes he forgot social graces like not drawing attention to one's wealth or lack thereof, and he always felt like an idiot for it. That was the trouble with growing up dirt poor. He never quite shrugged the street off himself.

"Yeah, I have sort of a view," she said.

"You live in this neighborhood?"

"Not too far," she said, walking away from the window to the dining room table, where the food was waiting. "This looks great," she said.

"Shall we?"

He pulled out a chair, and she sat. While they ate they chatted about business at Cabaret, getting Arianna's dance school started and Simon's art—two of his pieces hung in the living room.

By the end of dinner, Noah was surprised how easy and comfortable he felt with her, like old friends. Well, old friends who'd had sex, but still…

Arianna stood to go study one of Simon's black-and-white paintings.

"It's really good," she murmured. "Just beautiful."

He was watching her, not the painting. "You're beautiful," he said as he approached her.

She looked at him. He didn't really think it through. He kissed her. And this was a dangerous kiss, because he wasn't going to be able to walk away, or send her off into the night. Not this time. He wouldn't let it go down that way.

He was getting in deep with this kiss.

And she didn't push him away. Instead, she opened her lips, invited him in, flicked her tongue gently against his—a kiss that promised something more.

He pulled away, reluctant to break their connection. But he also didn't want to rush this. He didn't want to let lust dictate the course of the night. How to say that, though? The words wouldn't come, so the silence stretched.

The sudden awkwardness between them was torture after the ease with which they'd been talking a few minutes ago. He didn't quite know how to do this courting thing. Sex, he knew cold. He could go straight there, no problem. But when it came to all the other nuances of a relationship, he was pathetically out of his league, apparently.

His gaze fell on the edge of her tattoo that peeked out between where her top ended and her skirt sat low on her hip. Why had he never asked her about it before?

"Can I take a closer look at your tattoo?"

She glanced down at herself. "Oh, this? Sure." She lifted her top a bit to reveal a beautiful expanse of flat belly and curving hip, on which was drawn a branch of delicate cherry blossoms. A small black bird perched on the branch, gazing up toward an invisible sky.

"That's the prettiest tattoo I've ever seen," he said, and it was. Exquisite.

He'd never considered himself a fan of tattoos—until now. He could hardly tear his gaze away, but she lowered the bottom of her top, and he had no choice.

"Thanks, I got it a year ago."

"Does it have any personal symbolism?"

"Yeah, sort of."

"Anything you care to share?"

Her gaze went far away, to something outside the window. "Sure," she said, "but it's a long story, and maybe one you don't want to hear."

"Try me."

"MAYBE LATER." Ari hadn't come here to confess her deepest, darkest secrets.

She'd come here hoping for a chance to explore what she felt for Noah.

She could see in his gaze that he still wanted her sexually, and of course she still wanted him, too. Her appetite had only grown.

He didn't have to say anything. She could see it in his eyes, and she could feel it in his kiss and in the energy between them.

He slid his hand around her shoulder to her back, then up her neck and into her hair. When he pulled her close and kissed her again with all the urgency she'd expected, she had to face the battle between her desire and her wanting to slow down, to make this more than sex.

She broke their kiss and gave herself the space to take a deep breath and consider how to proceed. But her body—it was screaming for more.

"Are you okay?" Noah asked.

"Just a little keyed up," she said. "I forgot to breathe."

She laughed awkwardly at her stupid excuse, but he was too distracted by the matter at hand to be put off.

He frowned but simply returned to kissing her—this time trailing his lips along her forehead, down her temple, to her ear.

"You can breathe now, right?" he whispered.

"Sort of."

She wanted to tell him.

About the rape.

If he knew about that, he'd understand things about her that no one else did.

No, she didn't. That wasn't why she was here.

But maybe it was.

She'd never considered it before. But with his hands

roaming territory that he alone had explored in recent years, she felt as if she were a virgin starting all over again. This was all new to her again, this sharing of bodies and souls. She didn't know how to do it anymore, didn't know how to feel, how to love.

She didn't know this new version of herself, this virgin.

Yes, she wanted to tell him about the rape.

She had to tell him.

But now? Was there any better way to kill a mood?

Fear seized her as soon as she considered speaking about it aloud.

Ari focused on breathing. In, out, in, out…

His hands crept under her top, tracing her tattoo, reaching bare flesh, and she stiffened. He noticed.

"Is something wrong?"

"No," she lied, smiling to hide her fear.

"Are you sure?"

"I'm ticklish."

"Oh," he said, frowning, probably not quite buying it.

"It's okay," she whispered, then leaned in to kiss him and end the conversation.

Down low, against her abdomen, she could feel how ready he was to move things along.

Damn it.

Why did she have to choose this moment to get all serious and emotional?

Who was this version of her who couldn't even enjoy a carefree night with an attractive guy? Especially since she'd gotten busy with this man before. Was it being here? In the space where she'd hosted countless fantasies with Noah? Whatever it was, she didn't recognize herself anymore, almost as if she was looking into the mirror and seeing a stranger's face.

No, this wasn't her. She didn't know who she'd become, but it wasn't her.

His hands, exploring under her shirt again, found her breasts, and she considered forgetting herself and going straight for what they both wanted. He stopped kissing her when she hesitated.

"What is it?"

"I'm sorry," she said. "I can't do this."

He searched her gaze for an explanation, but she didn't have one, or at least not one she was willing to tell him.

"Did I do something wrong?"

"No. It's just…something I need to tell you."

"Okay," he said, withdrawing almost imperceptibly, so that she didn't feel his absence until there was a foot of space between them.

But she could see from his expression that he was a little freaked out and confused—exactly how she would have felt in his shoes.

"It's not you," she heard herself saying. "It's me."

Worst let-down line in the known universe, and she'd uttered it. Shame washed over her.

"Yeah," he said, trying to keep his tone light, but his smile was forced. "That's what they all say."

Apparently it wasn't what they all said to him, judging by the number of women she'd seen him bring home, but she couldn't exactly point that out.

"Could I get you a drink?" he asked.

"No, thanks."

This was it. It was her one and only chance to break out of the isolation she'd put herself in for the past two years, and she couldn't let fear get in her way now.

"I have to explain," she blurted, wondering what the hell

she thought she was going to say. "But maybe you're right—it would help to have a drink first."

He looked dubious, but he nodded and went to the kitchen.

"How about a scotch on the rocks?" he called out.

"Sure, thanks."

He brought their drinks and Ari downed hers as fast as she could.

Noah raised his eyebrows. "This must be a good story."

If he only knew. And what was she going to say? That she was a born-again virgin until she'd slept with him? That she'd intended to use him for sex, but then she'd realized she wasn't capable of casual sex anymore?

The psychological effect of the scotch hit her before the warm glow of actual inebriation did, and she felt herself relax by degrees. She settled back into the sofa and closed her eyes for a moment.

The ice in Noah's glass clinked, but he was otherwise silent. When she opened her eyes again, she found him watching her with a mixture of worry and curiosity.

Then the scotch really started to hit her, and she exhaled the tension in her body.

"I was raped," she said softly.

It came out so easily, so simply, she wasn't quite sure she'd said the words aloud, until Noah reacted.

His brow creased, and his gaze darkened. "When?"

"Just over two years ago."

Silence as he processed this bit of information.

"I haven't been with a man since," she added. "Until you."

"Oh," he said quietly.

All her weird behavior probably made sense to him now.

"It happened right outside the back door of the club—the one that leads to the alleyway. It was late, after closing, and everyone else had gone home. I was locking up when I was attacked."

"Was it someone you knew? Was he caught?"

Ari wanted to call an end to the question-and-answer session, but she knew this was progress. She was volunteering information she'd rarely told anyone, and she wasn't completely freaking out about it. Now was not the time to turn tail and run.

"I didn't know him, but I was able to ID him in a police lineup. He was convicted last year and sent to prison."

"Cold comfort, I imagine."

She nodded. "Yeah, but it's okay. I mean, I think I'd be a lot more freaked if he were still out wandering the streets."

"Sure, but I'd much rather feed the bastard to some hungry sharks than imagine him alive and well."

Ari was surprised by the anger in his tone. She'd lost the anger, at least, when the trial was done. Of course Noah was experiencing it all for the first time. The facts would take time to settle, and if he chose to stick around, he'd discover, too, that anger was too much of a burden to hold on to.

"I'm not angry about it much anymore. A year ago, I got the tattoo, as a gift to myself. Something beautiful, to make me happy when I look at it. Because too often I found myself looking in the mirror and hating the memories that came to me when I did."

"You should never hate what you see when you look in the mirror," he said softly.

The last thing she was expecting was for him to lean across the space between them and kiss her. This time, she didn't stop him. The burden off her shoulders, she wanted him now.

16

"I WANT YOU TO LIE DOWN and let me touch you for a while."

"What do you mean?"

"I just want to touch you."

"You don't have to be like my seeing-eye lover, you know," she said, but he laid her out on the wide white sofa and told her to relax.

He laughed. "Maybe I want to honor how amazing your body is. Consider it a ceremonial cleansing."

She sighed and lay all the way back. Actually, she loved the idea of him hovering over her, studying her like a sacred text.

"Do you like to be touched here?" he asked.

Arianna closed her eyes, her mind focusing on the feel of his fingertips trailing up her calf.

"Yeah."

He took his time, moving at an excruciatingly slow pace. Then his touch was gone.

Next, she heard him fiddling with a plastic lid, and she smelled something spicy and woodsy. "What's that scent?"

"Massage oil."

"You're going to give me a *massage?*"

"What could be slower than that?"

"A coma, maybe," she said, smiling.

"I thought a massage would be more fun."

"I agree."

She sighed as he began rubbing massage oil into her calf, finding tense spots she hadn't even realized existed.

He worked his way up her legs, maintaining a respectful distance from any truly erogenous zones, and Arianna had to give him credit—he was a great massage therapist.

He moved to her feet, then instructed her to roll over, and he began working on her back.

He worked so slowly and thoroughly, she was sure hours had passed by the time he finally reached her neck and shoulders. Yet when she glanced at the clock, she saw that it had only been about forty-five minutes.

The way he was touching her—it didn't feel sexual, and she didn't feel exactly aroused so much as relaxed. It was remarkable. He'd been touching her nonstop for almost an hour, and she was completely relaxed.

She still wanted him, but she was impressed by both of their abilities to remain in control.

He bent and kissed her shoulder, so gently she almost couldn't feel it, except for his breath tickling her skin. Maybe they wouldn't have sex at all.

"I want you to feel totally worshipped," he said. "Do you?"

"Yeah," she said with a sigh. "I do."

"Good," he said. "Now touch me."

She smiled as she let her hands travel over him, marveling at the real-life feel of the man who'd appeared in so many of her fantasies both real and imagined. She tugged his shirt from his pants, and beneath it her hand brushed hot flesh. She felt his chest and his back with a light tickling touch, enjoying the feel of his skin turning to gooseflesh.

Then she let her hand brush his jutting erection through his pants, and they were both done for.

She wanted him so badly she couldn't see straight, and she didn't want to take it slowly anymore.

"I want you inside me," she whispered, and before she knew it, he'd lifted her up from the couch and was carrying her across the room.

HE BACKED HER UP to the wall and slid his hand down her rib cage, over her hipbone, under her skirt and between her legs. She was wearing the thinnest, silkiest little scrap of underwear he'd ever felt. It almost wasn't there. He could feel her every contour through the panties. She was warm and growing wetter by the second as he stroked his fingers back and forth.

He'd missed this. He wasn't sure where he'd found the strength to stop having sex with her.

She had a dazed, aching look in her eyes. He knew how badly she wanted him, because he wanted her at least that much himself.

He wanted to bury himself inside her.

She kissed him, her tongue coaxing him farther and farther into her. And then he found his way to her neck, where he nipped and sucked until she was writhing against him.

He should have stopped right there. He thought of Dr. Chen and her warnings.

He was doing this all wrong. He was never going to be cured.

But this—Arianna—felt too right to be wrong. She was his salvation. In this moment, he was certain of it. Somewhere inside her lay the cure to everything that had ever gone wrong in his life.

He tugged her panties down, and she stepped out of them. Then he dropped to his knees and pushed her skirt up to her waist. Lifting one of her legs and propping it on his shoulder, he brought his mouth to her pussy and licked her gently until she was moaning and squirming against him.

He took his time, savoring the agony of it, bringing her to the edge of climax, then backing off, much to her frustration.

Finally, she grabbed him and tugged him back up. He pulled off her shirt, and she unfastened his belt and pants. Before he had a moment to reconsider, she had her hand around his hard cock, and he was lost.

No backing down now. No telling his stone-faced psychologist how he'd faced down temptation and conquered it. That woman knew nothing about temptation.

Now he was naked, pressing himself against Arianna as they kissed in a hungry frenzy, tasting and biting and licking at each other. He found a condom in his wallet and slid it on with fumbling hands, desperate to get on with the task at hand.

His cock jutted between her legs, and he lifted her up again. She wrapped her legs around him, so that he had no choice but to slide inside her. Her body, hot and wet, enveloped him, and every ache he'd ever had seemed to be eased in that moment.

But then a whole new level of aching began to build as he started moving inside her. She held tight to him, gasping in his ear as he pumped hard into her, faster and faster, harder and harder.

No more being gentle. No more taking things slowly. A dam had burst, and he poured forth like a raging river no longer restrained.

But this standing up, holding her against the wall, it wasn't enough. He needed to feel all of her against him, needed his hands free to explore and pleasure. So he lifted her again and carried her out of the living room and into his bedroom. He laid her down on the bed and climbed on top, covering her with his naked body and pushing himself back inside her immediately.

He was pumping into her again when he realized where they were.

On his bed.

He never brought women here.

Ever.

Sex happened in the living room, in the kitchen, on the dining room table, in the shower, or maybe bent over the bathroom counter. Never here.

This was his sanctuary, the place he came to escape.

But he didn't want to escape Arianna. He wanted *her* to be his refuge.

He slowed, then came to a stop, still inside her, still pulsing with need.

She squirmed beneath him, urging him to continue.

"Wait," he whispered.

"Is something wrong?"

"No."

"What is it, then?"

"I just want to take a minute so I can remember this."

He looked at her, really looked at her. He committed her to memory, exactly like this—dark hair a tangled halo around her face, cheeks flushed pink with desire, eyes wide and glazed, lips damp and parted. She was beautiful, and she was here with him, in his bed.

And he wanted her here. He felt safe with her. He felt like he was home.

This was a picture to recall when he was ninety and wanted to imagine the best moments of his life. It didn't get better than this.

"Noah?"

Her expression had changed from curious to worried. "What?"

"You're crying." She wiped at his cheeks, and he could feel the dampness then.

But he was the tough one. He wasn't supposed to cry. He took care of things. He didn't have the luxury of tears.

The emotions were below the surface, and they were bubbling up now. Here. Safe with her. He couldn't not allow himself to feel. Really feel.

"I love you," he said.

And it was true.

He did.

So this was what it felt like.

She was blinking at him, stunned. He put a finger to her lips.

"Shh," he said, and he began moving inside her again.

He rolled them so that she was on top, where he could touch her until she came. And with her above him, her heavy breasts swaying with each thrust, he almost couldn't hold himself off, but he managed—barely.

He slid his thumb along her clit, back and forth, softly, softly, and watched the tension build in her face before he could feel it in her pussy. She was almost there.

Almost, almost… And then she was, and her face crumpled in pleasure, and she cried out as she was overcome with the orgasm.

Then he was there with her, his body rocking him as he spilled into her.

She collapsed on top of him, gasping, and he listened as her breathing slowed. He could feel her heartbeat against his chest slowing, too.

After a few minutes, he could still feel his *I love you* hanging in the air between them.

"About what I said," he whispered.

"Noah—" she said as she pushed herself up to look him in the eye.

"Don't say anything," he said. "You don't need to feel the same. Just know that I—I haven't felt like this since…since ever."

She blinked. "You've never been in love before?"

"Not like this."

"But…"

"When you grow up like I did, you learn not to let anyone get too close. You go into survival mode, and you forget that there's more to life than surviving. You get hungry, and you eat too much, but you never learn to slow down and enjoy the food."

"What?"

"Sorry, that was a bad metaphor. I'm going to shut up now."

He shifted his hips, and she closed her eyes and gasped softly. And there wasn't anything more to say.

17

HE *LOVED* HER?

He loved her.

Ari tried to put that thought out of her head, but it wouldn't go away. It kept bubbling up, no matter what sort of divine things he was doing to her body.

He'd said he loved her, and it was the last thing she'd expected him to say.

Even worse, she could tell he meant it. And that he wasn't one of those guys who only said it when they were rolling around in the hay.

But then he'd rolled them both over, and she was on top, and he was holding his hips as he pumped into her from this new angle, and it was too damn perfect for her to have another negative thought.

Now that they were done, he began kissing her softly— her mouth, her face, her eyelids. Then he pulled her down to rest on his shoulder.

She'd never had such great sex in her life.

Spent, they both drifted off into a shallow sleep, and when Ari awoke a little while later, she'd lost the euphoria of their encounter. She wasn't even sure, for a moment, where she was.

Low-slung modern bed, with a pale teak headboard and a

thick, luxurious white duvet, cool gray-blue walls, a contemporary abstract painting on the wall…

It was all oddly familiar. Then she remembered. This was a place she'd only seen before through binoculars.

Noah's bedroom.

Come to think of it, on the occasions when he'd had his bedroom blinds open, she'd never seen any other woman in here. He didn't invite his lovers to stay. He did them in the window then escorted them out the door, as far as she could tell.

And here she was, lying in Noah's bed, his arm draped over her as he snored softly with his breath tickling the back of her neck.

He loved her.

She hadn't expected him to ever feel that—quite the opposite. She'd chosen him as a lover precisely because he never seemed to get heavily involved.

She wasn't sure she was even capable of falling in love again. And whatever she felt for Noah—lust, attraction, maybe a bit of friendly admiration for his accomplishments and his obvious affection for his brother—could it amount to love?

She'd thought that was exactly what she had come here to find out, but now that she was faced with the reality of it, she was terrified.

What did it mean to be loved by a man with a sex addiction? Would he love her and still sleep with a different woman every other night when she wasn't around?

How could she even continue here with him now, in good conscience, knowing he loved her and that she wasn't sure she could ever trust him?

She couldn't.

She couldn't have love without trust.

She'd have to break this off.

She was starting to feel normal and happy and stable again, and she couldn't risk upsetting that shaky sense of normalcy.

It was only fair that she break things off with Noah.

But he wasn't going to like it, especially not after tonight. He was going to take it badly. Which meant she needed to get this over with sooner rather than later.

She rolled over, and her movement woke him.

"Hmm?" he said, opening one eye.

"Noah, I need to talk to you."

Her tone caused his other eye to pop open. He was staring at her now, looking a little concerned.

"What is it?"

"About what you said a little earlier…"

A smile played on his lips. "The *I love you* part? Ari, don't let that freak you out, okay? It was heartfelt, but it doesn't mean I'm laying any expectations on you."

"Well, I understand, but it's not fair for me to know you're feeling that way and not acknowledge it, and explain where I'm coming from."

"Why don't you take a little time to process it. I know it's a big bomb to drop on someone who's not expecting it. It's just, I don't know if I've ever felt this good in my entire life, and I'm really grateful to you for helping me feel this way."

Oh God.

There couldn't be any putting this off. It was only going to hurt worse and worse the more she let him talk like that.

"Noah, stop, please. Let me say something."

"Sure," he said. "Go ahead."

"I'm not in love with you, and I'm not going to be."

"How do you know that?" he said, nonplussed.

"Because I know myself. And I know what I need to feel sane and okay right now, and it's not…this. It's not you."

Silence. He stared at her, expressionless for a moment, then he rolled onto his back and looked at the ceiling.

"I would have said the same thing a few months ago, so I think I know where you're coming from."

"It's not about you," she lied.

There it was again—the worst line in the known universe. Ashamed, she went silent, not sure what to say that would sound any less awful.

He smiled. "I would have said that, too."

"I'm a coward," she said. "I can't handle putting myself at risk right now. It's been too hard getting back to a place where I feel good about my life, and I'm terrified of losing that feeling."

He rolled back onto his side, propping his head on his elbow. "That makes sense," he said. "You have had a rough time, and if I were you I'd be terrified, too."

"You're not upset?"

"I'd rather you love me in return, but I love you enough to want whatever's best for you."

Maybe he'd lost his mind. Whatever was going on, he was definitely experiencing a little too much euphoria. Soon enough he'd get a grip on reality again and realize she was being a horrible shit.

"That's really generous of you," she said.

"Please, Ari—you can do whatever you want, but could you please stay here with me tonight?"

How could she say no to that?

She couldn't. So she stayed until right before dawn, and snuck out as the night slipped away.

NOAH STUMBLED THROUGH the next day in an aching stupor. So he'd discovered that he was capable of falling in love, and he'd discovered the pain of a broken heart, all on the same night.

And it hurt like hell once the initial euphoria wore off. He was sure at any moment he'd look down to see the gaping hole where vital organs had been ripped out. That actually might have been less painful.

He'd come home early from work because he'd felt so horrible. Collapsing in bed to sleep seemed the best way to not have to think about the fact that Arianna didn't love him. The ringing phone woke him, but it wasn't on the nightstand where it belonged.

He jumped out of bed in search of the handset. He normally wouldn't have bothered answering this late, but maybe it was Arianna calling to say she'd changed her mind—that she wasn't so averse to love or him loving her.

He finally found the phone on his kitchen counter and picked it up without looking at the caller ID.

"Hello?"

"Noah, baby, how are you?"

A female voice, but he couldn't place it.

"Who's this?" he asked.

"It's Jennifer. I'm in front of your building."

Jennifer?

"Oh. Well, it's kind of late," he said, as his mind raced to recall who Jennifer was.

Then he looked out his window down at the sidewalk and remembered. She was staring up at him, waving. He waved back.

Tall, blond, gorgeous curves, killer legs. Jennifer. They'd had a few incredibly hot nights together.

"It's been too long," she said. "I was in the neighborhood and thought I'd check to see if you could use a little company."

Jennifer was exactly the kind of lover he'd always liked. She didn't care about having a relationship. She only wanted sex, and lots of it.

Could he use a little company now?

He was alone. The woman he loved didn't love him back. And he had no reason to turn her down.

Old habits were easy to slip back into.

Frankly, the thought of another woman right now sounded about as appealing as a double root canal, but he needed to do something to distract himself from this horrible pain.

"Okay," he said without giving it any further thought. "Come up and have a drink."

"A drink?" she said, a smile in her voice. "Sure. I'll be right there."

He brushed his teeth and ran his fingers through his hair in place of a comb, then Jennifer was knocking on his door.

He opened it, and she opened up her coat to reveal that she wasn't wearing any clothes underneath.

Lush, full tits beckoned to him. And not far below them was a golden little triangle of curls that promised easy pleasures. Yeah, he remembered Jennifer. There weren't that many lovers he could say that about.

She'd been really, really good.

"Hi," he said, stepping aside for her to come in, his gaze lingering on her naked body.

He expected to feel a hot surge of desire.

But…nothing.

He felt nothing.

Except maybe the slightest little bit of revulsion.

She smiled. "Hi, yourself," she said as she entered and shrugged off her coat.

Now she wore nothing but a pair of black stiletto heels. The curves of her firm hips and ass caught his eye as she strutted across the room and tossed her coat on a chair.

Noah followed her. "Could I, um, get you a glass of wine?"

"I could do without the drink," she said. "Why don't you just come on over here and stick that nice big cock of yours in me?"

That was about as good an invitation as he'd ever gotten. He watched as she lay down on his sofa and propped one leg up. She slid her hands over her body, teasing at her nipples, stroking her clit, readying herself for him.

Still, he felt nothing. Not even a little bit aroused.

He thought of Arianna. Just a day ago she'd been here, and he'd felt such raging desire for her, he doubted he could have stopped himself from taking her if she'd told him no.

Now he had another woman inviting him to take her, and he felt the opposite.

Dr. Chen had been full of it. He didn't need to avoid sex. None of that mattered. What he needed was to forget all the psychobabble and live his life the way he best saw fit.

Maybe he needed a little coaxing where Jennifer was concerned—a little physical stimulation. He went to her and knelt beside the couch. He willed himself to reach out and slide his hand along the smooth expanse of her belly, but his muscles were frozen. He couldn't touch her.

She tilted her head back, closed her eyes and moaned softly as she continued stroking herself. "Come on," she whispered. "Give me what I want."

His body had no more response than if he was watching the morning stock reports.

This, frankly, scared the hell out of him. What kind of man was he if he couldn't be aroused by a beautiful woman wanting him to screw her brains out?

More coaxing. He was heartbroken, and apparently that messed with his sex drive.

Jennifer, sensing his lack of interest, opened her eyes and sat up. She faced him, spreading her legs and sliding herself forward until she was almost straddling his hips, but he stood and backed away before their bodies could touch.

She frowned. "You already do somebody else tonight?" she said. "You're a little spent, I can tell. Good thing that turns me on," she said with a wicked little smile. "I think I can still smell her on you."

He silently cursed himself. All he had to do was take out his cock and let her coax him into an erection, and he'd be well on his way to forgetting about Arianna.

Wouldn't he?

"Come back here," she said, her voice low and husky now.

He had zero desire to comply. And she sensed it.

"Do you want me to call a friend?" she said. "I know a few women who'd be happy to join us for a little threesome, if that's your thing."

Was that what he wanted? Would two women be able to do what one couldn't?

Any sane man would have said yes, but he shook his head.

No amount of empty stimulation was going to coax his flaccid cock into performing. And he was starting to feel a little embarrassed by the whole thing.

Only, it wasn't his lack of physical response that embarrassed him so much as it was her throwing herself at him this way.

Had he outgrown this sort of thing?

An image of Arianna popped into his head, and he had his answer.

He couldn't want anyone but her now.

He shook his head. "No," he said, "I'm sorry, but I can't. You have to go."

18

SHE'D PROMISED HERSELF she wouldn't watch him anymore. She'd promised, but apparently she had no willpower at all.

None, nada, zip.

Ari had expected escaping Noah's bed to bring some relief. She'd gotten over her fear of physical intimacy, and she'd made it out of her first relationship in a long time without any major scrapes or bruises.

Or so she'd thought. Because a day after walking out of Noah's apartment, she couldn't stop thinking about him, couldn't stop aching for him, couldn't stop remembering the good parts of having him in her life.

So when she'd been sitting in her living room in the dark staring out the window, and the light had come on in Noah's apartment, she couldn't help but notice what was going on.

Noah, bare-chested, going to his front door, opening it, talking to a tall blond woman whom Ari was pretty sure she'd seen there before… The woman, shrugging off her coat, naked beneath it, going to the couch, lying down… Noah, kneeling beside her…

At that point, Ari had considered picking up the binoculars, just to torture herself. She'd been stunned that he'd move on to a new lover so quickly. And yet, she'd been stupid to think he'd do anything else. She, of all people, knew what his revolving-door love life was like.

She couldn't watch anymore. She'd snapped the blinds shut, muttering angry curses to herself as she went to bed.

How could the bastard have done that? How could she have been so stupid? On and on the questions went.

Now, lying alone in her bed, knowing that Noah was with someone else, knowing that his tears yesterday had been a manipulative act, she couldn't sleep, couldn't stop reminding herself what a fool she was.

She'd broken her own rule. She'd wanted it to be only sex, then she'd gone and let herself get emotionally involved anyway.

She was such a goddamn fool.

She'd known all along what kind of guy Noah was. It shouldn't have been any surprise that it had only taken him twenty-four hours to replace her.

He was doing what he'd always done.

She should have been glad he wasn't sulking, glad he wasn't plotting to get her back, glad he'd moved on.

But she wasn't any of those things.

WHEN ARI HEARD Noah's voice on the phone two days later, her first reaction was to hang up. But before she could, he said, "It's Simon."

Noah's words were so upsetting, she only caught phrases: "suicide attempt," "distraught over things not going well with Sophie" and "he's asking to see you." And in a matter of minutes she was in her car, driving as fast as she could to the hospital.

When she found Simon in his hospital room, he looked like hell from having had his stomach pumped and some kind of black stuff forced into him that had stained his mouth.

"Simon, my God," she whispered. "Don't do that."

He gazed up at her with sleepy, disoriented eyes. "Ari… You came to see me."

"Of course I did," she said.

"Why?"

"Shh," she said, sitting on the edge of his bed.

"Why do you even give a damn about me?"

Arianna felt tears welling up in her eyes. She tried to speak but found her voice choked. "Because I do. I think it's a birds-of-a-feather thing."

"You mean you're crazy, too?"

"Maybe not in the diagnosable sense, but I mean…some of us have stuff bottled up, painful stuff, and it's easy for me to see it in someone else."

"You ever tried to kill yourself?"

Arianna shook her head, and now that he'd spoken the awful words out loud, the tears spilled, drenching her cheeks.

"Don't ever do that again."

Simon laughed. "Turns out I'm not very good at it, anyway. Is there anything worse than being a failure at dying?"

"Being a success is definitely worse."

He sighed. "Yeah. Maybe."

"Did you really do this over Sophie?" She was almost too afraid to ask, but she had to know.

Simon, unable to meet her eyes, just nodded.

"Oh, Simon. What happened?"

"She broke up with me."

Ari recalled Noah's warnings, and now her own stupidity struck her like a punch to the gut. God, why hadn't she listened to him? Why hadn't she been able to trust that he would know better than her what was right for his brother?

Because she was a stubborn fool.

"Did you two get in a fight or something?"

"Not exactly. She just… She said she only wants to be friends. And I don't."

"She's afraid. Give her time. She'll come around," Ari said, then wanted to kick herself. She needed to stop meddling.

Ari looked up when a movement outside the door of the hospital room caught her eye. It was Sophie, waiting to see Simon. She was crying.

"I have something to confess," Simon said.

"Yeah?"

"I know you live in the building across from Noah's."

Oh God.

Oh, dear God.

"You do?" Ari croaked.

"Yeah, I mean, every once in a while you'd have your blinds up, and I could see you dancing around in your apartment."

No.

"You could?"

He looked a little embarrassed. "Yeah, and…I made a painting of you."

"You did?" she said, stunned.

This was far better than him accusing her of being a Peeping Tom.

"I want to give it to you, I mean, if you want it. I don't know if it's any good."

"Wow, Simon. Thank you. I'd be honored."

"Don't thank me until after you see it. You might hate it."

"I can't wait to see it," she said. "I'm sure I'll love it, because you painted it." She leaned over to kiss his forehead. "Someone else is waiting to see you."

Simon followed Ari's gaze to the door, to Sophie, who smiled tentatively at him through her tears.

Time for Ari to bow out.

FROM THE HOSPITAL'S meditation garden, Noah stared up at the night sky—a rare clear night, barely twinkling with stars that competed with the light from the city. This was what it felt like to be alone in a city full of people. It was a feeling he should have been used to by now.

"Thank God he's okay," he said to no one in particular.

He heard a movement from behind him, and turned to find Arianna standing there.

"He's lucky to have you as a brother, you know."

Noah looked over at her. He was glad to see her, even if she had broken his heart.

"Simon," he said slowly, "is a lot like our mother was, before she died."

"How so?" she asked.

"Our mother was mentally ill, bipolar like Simon, only she wouldn't take her medication most of the time."

"That must have been hard for you both."

"She killed herself."

"Oh, Noah. I'm so sorry."

He was startled at the empathy in her tone. He never told this story to anyone, but when he imagined telling it, he always pictured his listener recoiling at the ugliness of it.

He should have known Arianna wouldn't be cruel enough to do that. But still, she must have been inwardly horrified.

Her gaze communicated the same feeling as her tone, though, and Noah looked away, afraid of the raw feelings between them.

"Don't be. It's all in the past."

"How did it happen?"

Noah took a deep breath. He didn't think about the particulars of his mother's death anymore. "She hated the side effects of her meds, so she'd stop, thinking she could handle the mood swings, or that they wouldn't come back."

"And then they would."

"Yeah. She went into a downward spiral when I was a senior in high school, and one day a lifeguard found her washed up on the beach. She couldn't swim, and she'd gone out onto the Venice Beach pier and jumped off."

"What happened to you and Simon?"

"We were on our own."

"There was no other family to look out for you?"

"Nope. Mom was a hippie, ran away from an abusive family back in Ohio and never spoke to them again. One time child protective services tried to track down some relatives to see if anyone might help us out, but no one was willing, far as I know."

"It must have been horrible for both of you." She was shaking her head, frowning, and starting to shiver from the cold night air.

Noah took off his jacket and placed it over her shoulders, and to his surprise she didn't protest.

That one little acceptance of his caring gesture left him feeling split wide open, breathless with the ache in his chest.

"I'm not telling you any of this to make you feel sorry for me."

"I know that."

"I mean, my past is what it is. And in some ways it was a gift to have something to struggle against growing up. It taught me how to be a survivor."

"It takes a pretty remarkable person to overcome what you did and become such a success in life," she said.

"I don't know about that. But I do know Simon isn't quite as resilient as I am. That's why I can be a little overprotective. I'm sorry I didn't explain it to you sooner."

"No, I'm sorry. You know what's best for your brother better than I do, and I should have listened to you."

Noah shook his head. "Please don't feel responsible. Simon's an adult, after all. He doesn't want either of us trying to orchestrate his life for him.

"I'm plagued with feeling like if I'd somehow done something different, Simon would be more okay than he is, and our mother might still be alive."

"Don't do that to yourself. It's not fair."

"I know. And sometimes I'm relieved my mom's not around to take care of anymore."

She regarded him seriously. "Those are natural feelings, you know. Nothing to be ashamed of."

"Part of me didn't want to take care of her anymore. But right now I do wish she was around. I'd be able to get her a place, and she wouldn't have to live on the street ever again."

When he looked at Ari again, she was blinking away tears and looking at him as if he'd spoken some magic words.

"Believe me, I know how it feels to wish you could change the past. I tell myself, 'If only I'd left the building earlier that night,' or 'If only I'd carried a bottle of pepper spray.'"

"The night you were raped," he said, forcing himself to speak the ugly word. It was a fact about Ari he couldn't change, and it only made him love her more. She'd endured something painful and found a way to survive and even thrive, rather than letting it ruin her. He admired that about her.

"Yes," she said. "And there's no more futile wish in the universe, far as I can tell, than to wish to change the past. Please don't torture yourself with it."

"You're right."

"Maybe sometimes, it's okay to let someone else take care of you, too, instead of you always being the caregiver."

She turned away from the railing and walked to a bench beneath a flickering outdoor security light. There, she sat and stared at her feet for a moment before looking up at Noah again and patting the space next to her.

"Sit," she said. "As long as we're exchanging deep dark secrets, there's something I have to tell you."

"Yeah?" he said as he sat.

"I recognized you, when I first saw you at Cabaret."

"Where from?"

"We're neighbors. I live in the building across from yours."

He frowned, trying to recall ever having seen Arianna before, but he couldn't. "You do?"

"Yeah." Her expression seemed tortured.

"So? We've passed on the street?"

"Not that I know of. I knew you because I used to watch you. From my living room window. I used to watch you with your lovers."

Damn. He should have known in such a relatively small city—geographically small, anyway—his Lothario behavior would catch up with him sooner or later.

Finally, the Sir Sex-a-Lot comment he'd heard between her and Kip made sense. He'd thought they'd been talking about how often he and Ari'd had sex, but now...

Noah laughed and felt his cheeks redden. "You must have gotten quite a show."

"I did," she said quietly, her gaze cast downward.

"I...I'm a little embarrassed, I admit."

"So am I."

"I'm sorry." For what? For being an exhibitionist? For sleeping with too many women? For living across the street from her apartment?

"Don't be. If I hadn't wanted to see the show, I could have closed my blinds. But I used to watch. A lot. I mostly stopped after we met, but there are a few times..."

Noah laughed a nervous laugh. "So you're a voyeur and I'm an exhibitionist. Does that mean we make the perfect match, or a fatally flawed one?"

Her weak smile did little to soothe his nerves. "I'm not really a voyeur. I'd never watched anyone before…"

"Before what?"

Silence. Then she glanced over at him, her face pale.

"Before the rape. After…I don't know, maybe a year, I noticed you out my window one night, going at it with some woman, and…"

"It turned you on?"

She nodded. "It was the first time I'd felt any real sexual desire. I'd been worried my body had shut down and wouldn't ever feel that way again."

"So I guess it's kind of a good thing I was there in the window," he said, half joking.

"I guess it was. I mean, I got off on watching. And if it weren't for you, I might still be unable to enjoy sex."

"It's a pretty weird coincidence that we ended up lovers, don't you think?"

Her cheeks turned red. "It wasn't exactly a coincidence. When I recognized you, I decided then and there that you'd be the first man I had sex with after the rape."

"I'm…honored."

But was he? Had she really pursued him solely for sexual purposes? And if so, why did he even care, when that's what he'd done to countless other women?

He didn't have any right to care, but he did.

He wanted her to want him for real, not just for sex.

"You're not offended?"

"How could I be, when I was the one putting myself out there—literally?"

Ari shrugged, then frowned. "Why did you?"

Good question. Noah hadn't ever forced himself to face the answer. He knew that he'd gotten a little too compulsive in the sex department, but he didn't know the answer to Ari's question until he opened his mouth and it came out.

"I guess it was a sort of conspicuous consumption thing. I wanted the world to see how good my life was, after having spent so much of my life on the wrong side of the window looking in, with things going so badly."

To his relief, she smiled. "I guess public sex is better than driving a Maserati."

"You must think I'm a total man-whore."

"Actually," she said, her expression growing darker. "I was watching you two nights ago, and I definitely shouldn't have been."

Jennifer. "Ari, don't think—"

"It's none of my business."

"She showed up out of the blue. I was brokenhearted, and thought I could use the distraction. But I didn't want her there. I sent her away before anything happened."

"You did?"

"Didn't you see?"

"I stopped watching when you knelt in front of her."

"It didn't go any further than a peep show, Ari. Please believe that."

Silence, for a painfully long time, during which Noah contemplated the cruel twist of fate that would make her stop watching before he finally found a scrap of nobility left inside his slimy self.

"Do you think you're capable of being monogamous?" she finally asked.

Noah laughed in spite of himself. "Capable of being

monogamous? With you? You'd turn the most devoted player into a one-woman man."

"My ego thanks you, but seriously. Do you?"

He sobered, understanding her worry. "Of course I am. It's only been in the past few years that I've overindulged."

"I really can't think you're a man-whore when I'm no angel, either."

"What do you mean?"

"Aside from being the one watching you, I was a wee bit insatiable myself back in the day."

"Before the attack?"

He would have hated to come upon the perpetrator in a dark alley, because Noah was quite sure he'd have to kill the man. He liked to think of himself as nonviolent and evolved, but some things were best handled with brute force—according to his gut, anyway.

The fierce protectiveness he felt for Ari didn't surprise him anymore. He understood it was there because he loved her, which made it his responsibility to protect her at all costs.

"Yeah. I had plenty of fun, and plenty of lovers. Maybe not all in my living room window…"

"Which is probably a good thing."

Irrationally, his stomach knotted at the idea of Ari having *plenty of fun* with *plenty of lovers. He* wanted to be the only man in the world for her, Neanderthal as the notion might have been.

And yet he knew, with a woman as amazing as her, he was lucky to get to be her man at all. If he could even call himself that.

"Thank you," he said before he forgot himself.

"For what?"

"For befriending Simon. For showing me what a great place Cabaret is. For reminding me what it feels like to be alive."

She stared at him, speechless.

"I say that at the risk of sounding hopelessly sappy, I know."

A slow smile brightened her face. "You do sound a little sappy."

"Can you respect me in the morning?" he joked, before he realized the question was an all-important one.

Almost as much as he wanted her love, he craved her respect. The world's respect, really. But most important Arianna's.

She cocked her head to the side and gave him a long look. "I really do respect you, you know. You're a good man, Noah."

He chuckled, uncomfortable under her scrutiny now that they were getting to the heart of things.

She leaned forward and placed her hand over his. "I do."

"After everything?"

"Yes."

"Why?" He should have simply said *thank you,* or *that's so nice of you to say,* or anything other than what he actually said.

"How could I not respect you? You're the most caring, driven, intelligent, passionate person I've ever met."

He let her words fill him up, finding all those empty little spots he'd been trying to cover for so long.

Sure, he shouldn't have needed any external validation. Sure, he knew he was a human being worthy of respect and love.

Sure he knew.

Sort of.

About as well as a first-time tight-rope walker knew he wouldn't get hurt falling into the net.

There was knowing, and then there was *knowing*.

Something about having Ari's approval gave him that extra boost of confidence he felt like he'd been looking for his entire life.

He took her hands in his and tugged her forward into his arms. Then he kissed her long and deep, making sure she felt everything he couldn't put into words.

After a while, he broke the kiss and looked at her, their faces still close. "I love you, Ari. You know that, don't you?"

She smiled. "I guess I do."

"You guess?"

"I love you, too," she said quietly.

Noah understood what a momentous thing that admission was. Ari, who'd spent the past few years protecting herself from everyone and everything, never letting anyone close, had allowed him into her heart.

And that was exactly where he intended to stay.

Epilogue

"IT'S NO FAIR THAT I don't get to wear a bridesmaid dress."

Ari eyed Kip over her shoulder as he zipped up the gown. "You look much better in a suit. You're pretty, but not *that* pretty."

"I didn't realize you were so narrow-minded."

"Five minutes," Cara called out through the studio door, and Ari's stomach pitched.

Holy cow.

Five minutes.

She cast a terrified look at Kip. Sophie, reapplying her makeup in the mirror, giggled.

Five minutes until Ari's wedding began, and she was so scared she could hardly breathe.

She stood in front of the wall mirror and took a long look at herself. She looked like…a bride. She wore an elaborate wreath of flowers on her head, and a simple white calf-length gown that hugged her curves.

Sophie's phone beeped. "Oh, it's Simon," she said, opening up the phone and reading a text. "He says he wants to know when our wedding is going to be."

"How romantic—a texted proposal."

Except it was kind of romantic, since he'd been asking Sophie the same question nearly every other day since Noah and Ari had announced their own engagement three months ago. Sophie was slowly coming around to the idea, now that Simon had spent nearly a year stable, happy, employed and in love with her.

Ari was entirely convinced that Sophie's love was what kept him doing so well.

"Okay, people," Kip said. "Time for us to head downstairs."

This was her wedding procession—Cara, Kip and Sophie. They went downstairs and through the back door of Cabaret. When the wedding march began, they entered the main restaurant, which had been transformed into a wedding wonderland for the occasion. Ari looked around at the roomful of her friends.

Her family.

Up ahead, on the stage, stood Noah, Simon and Tyson.

Noah looked so handsome, so right, standing there waiting for her. She never had to view him from afar anymore, but seeing him now, with a bit of perspective, reminded her how far she'd come. She was no longer watching life happen. She was living it.

Ari's gaze met Noah's, and her nervousness faded away. She had never felt so sure about anything as she did about loving him.

Today was the day to tell the world how she felt.

HARLEQUIN
60
YEARS
of pure reading pleasure

We'll be spotlighting a different series
every month throughout 2009
to celebrate our 60th anniversary.

Look for Silhouette® Nocturne™ in October!

Travel through time to experience tales
that reach the boundaries of life and death.
Bestselling authors Lindsay McKenna, Cindy
Dees, P.C. Cast and Merline Lovelace join
together in a brand-new, four-book
Time Raiders miniseries.

TIME RAIDERS

nocturne™

New York Times bestselling author
and co-author of the House of Night novels

P.C. CAST

makes her stellar debut
in Silhouette® Nocturne™

THE AVENGER

Available October wherever books are sold.

TIME RAIDERS
miniseries

**Bestselling authors Lindsay McKenna,
Cindy Dees, P.C. Cast and Merline Lovelace
come together to bring to life incredible
tales of passion that reach the boundaries
of life and death, in a brand-new
four-book miniseries.**

Silhouette®

SPECIAL EDITION

FROM *NEW YORK TIMES* BESTSELLING AUTHOR

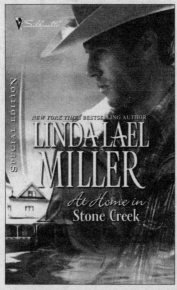

Ashley O'Ballivan had her heart broken by a man years ago—and now he's mysteriously back. Jack McCall *isn't* the person she thinks he is. For her sake, he must keep his distance, but his feelings for her are powerful. To protect her—from his enemies and himself—he has to leave...vowing to fight his way home to her and Stone Creek forever.

Available in November wherever books are sold.

Visit Silhouette Books at www.eHarlequin.com

SSE65487

Touch Me

by *New York Times* bestselling author
JACQUIE D'ALESSANDRO

After spending ten years as a nobleman's mistress,
Genevieve Ralston doesn't have any illusions
about love and sex. So when a gorgeous stranger
suddenly decides to wage a sensual assault on her,
who is she to stop him? Little does she guess he'll
want more than her body....

Available October wherever books are sold.

red-hot reads

www.eHarlequin.com

HB79499

You're invited to join our Tell Harlequin Reader Panel!

By joining our new reader panel you will:

- Receive Harlequin® books—they are FREE and yours to keep with no obligation to purchase anything!
- Participate in fun online surveys
- Exchange opinions and ideas with women just like you
- Have a say in our new book ideas and help us publish the best in women's fiction

In addition, you will have a chance to win great prizes and receive special gifts! See Web site for details. Some conditions apply. Space is limited.

To join, visit us at

www.TellHarlequin.com.

REQUEST YOUR FREE BOOKS!

2 FREE NOVELS PLUS 2 FREE GIFTS!

HARLEQUIN®

Blaze™

Red-hot reads!